THE BLACK DRAGON CAFE

THE BLACK DRAGON CAFE

CHINLE MILLER

Yellow Cat
PUBLISHING

Cover by Cary Cox. End photo by Chinle Miller.

For Viddy
And for Jim Waggoner

~

1

Bud Shumway kicked back in his leather recliner, half-dozing while wishing his wife, Wilma Jean, would get home before he starved to death.

He knew there was plenty to eat in the fridge, but he also knew she would be bringing leftovers from her cafe, which were usually much more tasty than whatever he could conjure up, which typically amounted to either a bowl of cereal or maybe some vanilla-bean ice cream if he felt particularly daring, knowing she would object if she found out.

Their three dogs slept on the floor by his feet, and he knew they would alert him when his wife's big pink Mary Kay Lincoln Continental came up the drive to their bungalow.

How dogs could be so alert when asleep was one of the many mysteries in life he'd decided he would never solve, along with things like why all roads lead to Rome, if zebras have black stripes on white or vice versa, and where watermelons originally came from. The latter mystery was a bit more pertinent, as he was a part-time watermelon farmer, as well as the Emery County Sheriff.

The dogs suddenly jumped up and ran to the door, tails wagging, and Bud knew Wilma Jean was home, even though he'd heard nothing. Going to the door and letting the dogs out, he could see his wife getting out of her car, though she didn't seem to be carrying anything except her purse.

Worried, Bud walked out onto the lawn in his socks, opening the front gate, the dogs following. Sure enough, Wilma Jean had none of the usual warming trays filled with stuff like spaghetti and meatballs, enchiladas, and chili.

Feeling a sinking feeling, Bud asked, "Is there stuff on the back seat to bring in?"

Wilma Jean, looking tired, replied, "Hon, I'm sorry, but we sold out of everything. I can't believe the crowd that came in. There's some kind of event in town, and nobody informed me so I could plan ahead. I actually had to close the cafe down early. Were you aware of anything going on?"

"No," Bud replied sorrowfully. "It's my day off. Nobody mentioned anything to me. I wonder if Howie knew."

"I suspect Howie's the reason all these people showed up. Maureen said it was some kind of art show. I'm going to give him an earful and remind him that as mayor if he doesn't let the townsfolk know what's going on, we can't properly serve our customers, and people probably won't come back."

"Do you think it's part of his new economic development push? He sure has the town divided on that one," Bud said, following his wife into the house, the dogs running ahead into the kitchen.

Howard McPherson, AKA Howie, had once been Bud's deputy and had then graduated to sheriff, replacing Bud, who wanted to farm melons, the stress of the job getting to him. But Howie had recently been elected mayor, and Bud had now stepped back in as sheriff, hiring a farm manager to make things easier. Bud often wondered if the state of Utah had ever had a sheriff who moonlighted as a watermelon farmer—or was it the other way around?

Wilma Jean replied, "Well, he sure irritated a lot of us when he decided to try to get a Cracker Barrel to come in. He almost got hung over that one, and I don't understand it, since it would be direct competition for his own drive-in. He's been taking his mayor job way too seriously and needs to go back to focusing on his rockabilly nights. Green River doesn't need any more cafes."

"Agreed, but I thought his idea of bringing in a chocolate factory was a good one," Bud said.

"They'd have trouble finding enough employees for a factory in a town this small," Wilma Jean replied. "Even though I know you'd probably sign up. But hon, someone left this by the cash register."

She took a small brown manila envelope from her purse and handed it to Bud. Handwritten on the front were the words, *Sheriff Shumway.*

Bud took the envelope and carefully opened the metal clasp. A folded piece of off-white, nubby paper fell out, made from what looked like parchment or some kind of watercolor paper.

Carefully holding it up, he noted it had an unusual slit in the front. Looking closer, he could see that a thin slice of the letter had been pushed through the slit and closed with a red wax seal, making it so the letter couldn't be opened without ripping the thin slice and breaking the seal, which would show that it had been tampered with.

He could make out the words on the wax seal: *Firmum in vita nihil.*

Holding the folded letter, Bud sat down at the kitchen table and sighed, his intuition telling him not to unseal it. For some reason, he sensed it could hold information he'd rather not know, something that could possibly turn his thoughts from having a late dinner to more serious matters.

"What is it?" Wilma Jean asked, looking over his shoulder.

"Some kind of letter, cleverly folded and sealed so I would know if someone else had opened it."

Bud took his pocket knife from his pocket and held the letter up, not really sure where to start. It then occurred to him that he should maybe have it fingerprinted before doing anything, just in case.

He was being silly, he mused, for it was probably just someone's idea of a joke, or maybe an elaborate invitation to a wedding—probably Frosty Merriott and Eileen Jensen's, which was coming up soon, assuming they didn't elope.

He carefully slid the knife under the wax, removing the seal. It took some doing to open the letter, as it had been folded inside itself several times, but when he finally got it open, he could see the writing was apparently done using a quill pen with black ink, some of which had smeared a little, as if the writer hadn't had the patience to let it dry before folding it.

Wilma Jean, watching over his shoulder, said, "Wow! That's some fancy handwriting."

Bud began reading out loud:

> The perfect crime,
> Will soon be committed.
> You won't know it happened,
> No sleuthing permitted.
> There won't be a body,
> No suspects, nor clues.
> This letter you're holding,
> Your only news.
> Iris and wheatfields,
> Starry skies filled with crows.
> Missing ears and letters,
> So life and death goes.
> —Yer pal, Vinnie

Wilma Jean said, "Bud, that's really odd. Sounds like Vincent van Gogh—*Starry Skies* is one of his most famous paintings, as is *Wheatfield with Crows*. And he loved to paint iris."

"What about the letters part?"

"Vincent van Gogh was famous for writing hundreds of letters, mostly to his brother Theo. He was prolific, and the letters are well-known for giving insight into the life of a tortured artist."

"How do you know so much about him?" Bud asked.

"We just read a book about him in my book club. It was totally tragic—and depressing."

Bud thought for a moment, then asked, "Why would someone

send me a letter like this? It doesn't even make sense. And to hand write it and go to all the trouble to seal it up like this..."

"They obviously didn't want anyone else to read it," Wilma Jean replied.

"But it doesn't even have any information in it," Bud said. "Except for the name Vinnie."

"Well, it does mention a crime, but it says you won't know it happened," Wilma Jean replied.

"And no clues," Bud said. "But just what exactly is a perfect crime?"

"I would guess one where no one knows a crime's been committed," Wilma Jean replied. "Kind of paradoxical to send a letter about it, though. But it's late. I need to get some rest, especially if tomorrow's going to be anything like today."

"What was going on exactly?" Bud asked. "I mean, I know you said it was an art show..."

"From the conversations I overheard, it sounds like Green River's been invaded by artists. And it seems like this letter is something an artist would send, mentioning Van Gogh. But hon, it's probably just a joke. Take the dogs out, then come to bed."

Bud stood and carefully folded the letter back up, placing it back in the brown envelope and putting it into the buffet drawer, along with the wax seal. He called the dogs, taking them out into the back yard.

There, he stood for awhile, wondering why someone would send him such a cryptic letter. Looking up, he could see a million diamond-like stars glittering in the deep-blue sky—kind of like a Van Gogh painting, he mused. After a few moments, he took the dogs back inside.

Wishing he'd listened to his intuition and waited until morning to open the envelope, he slipped the dogs each a Barkie Biscuit, then headed for the kitchen. He'd make himself a bowl of cereal, then go to bed, though he knew thinking about the letter would probably make it hard to sleep.

Whoever had written it must not know him very well to say no sleuthing permitted, for as sheriff, he was a natural sleuth—or were they maybe taunting him? But he knew it would be impossible to figure it all out if it truly was a perfect crime, for a perfect crime must be, by definition, undetectable.

Cereal finished, he slipped into his Scooby Doo PJs, then helped little dachshund Pierre onto the bed, who promptly crawled down under the covers. Their Basset hound, Hoppie, jumped up beside Wilma Jean, who seemed to already be asleep, while Lindie, a Carolina Dingo, turned around several times, then collapsed into her big plush dog bed on the floor near Bud.

Crawling into bed, Bud was careful to not let his cold feet touch his wife's leg, as he didn't want to get whacked on the head, experience being a good teacher.

"G'night," Bud whispered, then settled under the fluffy down comforter, again wondering who'd sent the letter and what it all meant.

2

"What exactly *is* a perfect crime, Howie?"

Bud was leaning back with his feet up, just like the previous night before Wilma Jean had come home, the main difference now being that he was in his office with his feet on his desk, and Mayor Howie sat across from him, thumbing through a week-old copy of the *New York Times*.

"Are you thinking of doing something you shouldn't, Sheriff?" Howie grinned. "If so, you've already blown it by mentioning it to me. The perfect crime is unnoticed, and the perpetrator is never caught."

"So, you've heard of the concept before?" Bud asked, now fiddling with a stapler.

Howie replied, "I read about an almost-perfect crime once when this guy tried to kill himself. He jumped off a big cliff, but he didn't know there was a net set up below for rock mitigation, so he would've landed in that and wouldn't have died, but on the way down, a gun went off from a nearby camp, and the stray bullet killed him."

"Wow, that's really odd," Bud replied. "But how would that be an almost-perfect crime?"

"Well, it seems that the bullet was from a gun which he himself owned. Someone went into his nearby tent and found it, and it accidentally went off just as this guy whizzed by on his way off the cliff. So instead of killing himself, he murdered himself, because he shouldn't have left the gun loaded, and he wouldn't have died otherwise."

"That's almost unbelievable, Howie. Are you sure that really happened?"

"No, it's just something I read. It could've been a plot someone was working on for a mystery. I guess it's an almost-perfect crime in that the guy was murdered and the murderer got away with it, even though he died."

"But there would be a body and all that, so not quite perfect," Bud said. "But Howie, whoever came up with that might want to reconsider their profession, as everyone knows a good mystery writer has to have a credible plot, one the reader can follow. You can't just throw things out willy nilly—well, you can, but people are going to say your plots don't take themselves too seriously."

"Yeah, I guess, but everyone knows it's the journey that counts, Sheriff. And you can't have a murder mystery without a murder, because at that point it's just a mystery. But why are you asking about the perfect crime, if you don't mind my asking?"

"I got this strange letter last night, saying the perfect crime was about to be committed."

"Did they say what kind of crime?"

"No, just a crime. But it did say there won't be a body, so I assumed it wouldn't be a murder."

"If they said there's no body, then it's definitely not a murder. Murders involve bodies. Can't go making assumptions in this business, Sheriff," Howie replied. "But maybe it was something minor, like robbing the bubble-gum machine down at the Chow Down. That would be a crime, and if you did it right, nobody would be the wiser except the guy who owns the machine, and he probably has it happen often enough he wouldn't bother to report it. That's an example of an almost-perfect crime. You get away with it, though it *is* noticed. But if you only stole a few bubblegums..."

"I'm sure it's happened before, Howie. But what does *Firmum in vita nihil* mean? The letter had those words on the seal."

"Well, all I know is *vita* means life, and *nihil* is probably like annihilate, so it probably means something like murder, you know, annihilate life, so maybe you're wrong about it not being a murder. *Firmum* would mean to be firm, to be sure you want to do it. Look it up."

Bud booted up his laptop and was soon doing an Internet search. Finally, he replied, "Close, but no cigar, Mayor. It means nothing in life is permanent."

"Murder's an impermanent thing, Sheriff. First you're here, then you're not, though I guess the ending's kind of permanent."

"Granted," Bud replied. "The letter was signed by someone named Vinnie. Do you know a Vinnie?"

"Susan Pratt's kid. He's the one who broke the window over at the hardware store. He has a good start to a life of crime. He very well could be one to steal bubble gum."

Bud replied, "I don't know, Howie. He got in a lot of trouble and had to work at the store after school till it was paid for. He has a regular part-time job there now after school. But the writing was very artistic, like with a quill pen. I doubt if he could write something like that."

"Maybe Susan wrote it for him."

Bud laughed. "If you knew Susan—she wanted me to put him in jail for a day to teach him a lesson, but I think he's learned what he needs to know at this point."

Bud again leaned back, then sighed. "But who carries a seal around with them these days? That's something from hundreds of years ago, when they didn't have envelopes and wanted to secure a letter. And you need wax and something to melt it with, like a lighter."

"Maybe a wax crayon, Bud. Something Vinnie Pratt might have handy."

Bud laughed as Howie continued. "Vinnie's a good Mafia name, Sheriff. I rest my case."

"Howie, Vinnie's short for Vincent, right?"

"It is."

"As in Vincent van Gogh?"

"Was he in the Mafia, Bud?"

"I doubt it—he was Dutch. I'm not even sure if there was a Mafia back then, especially a Dutch one."

"Look it up, Sheriff. We may be onto something here. Maybe they're the ones who cut off his ear."

Bud asked, "Say, are you aware that bringing a Cracker Barrel to Green River would hurt the business at your own drive-in?"

Howie groaned. "I've heard all about that, Bud. You should come over to my office and listen to my answering machine. I got a lot of flak over that one—both the East Winds and West Winds truck stops, the Willows Restaurant, even your wife. It was kind of Maureen's idea. She likes their shops—you know, while you're waiting for dinner, you can walk around and buy all kinds of junk. I didn't think it through very well, I admit."

"Why doesn't she just open her own shop? We actually could use one here. It might keep my wife from driving to Price all the time."

"Maureen's too busy covering for your wife at the Melon Rind when she goes to Price, plus taking care of little Malcolm and helping me with the drive-in. She'd rather shop than run one. But say, Bud, there's something I've been wanting to ask you about."

Howie hesitated, then continued. "Do you think it would help business if I renamed Howie's Drive-In to Mayor Howie's Drive-in? I mean, there's the Mayor's House B&B down in Radium. That's where I got the idea."

Bud grinned. "Howie, if I remember right, that business is just a few blocks over from Peggy Sue and Hum's place and actually is in the house a previous mayor built. The words mayor and drive-in kind of don't go together in my mind, but I guess you could give it a shot. It might work. But I thought you guys were already so busy you could barely keep up."

"We are," Howie replied. "Which reminds me, I need to get over there. You know, Sheriff, I like hanging around with you solving crimes. Sometimes I wish I'd never run for mayor."

"If you hadn't, you'd still be sheriff and I'd be a full-time melon farmer, so we still wouldn't be hanging around together all that much."

"True," Howie said, standing to go. "What I liked best was when you were sheriff and I was your deputy. But you know you can call me any time you need help solving anything."

"Even a perfect crime?" Bud grinned.

"Especially a perfect crime," Howie replied. "That would give me lots of time to hang out. But here come Molly and Kale. Do they come by very often?"

"No, almost never," Bud replied with concern. "Kale always calls if there's something on the farm he needs help with."

As Howie sat back down, Bud offered, "Maybe you should stick around for a minute and see what's going on. Maybe they're here to report a crime or something I could use your help with."

As Bud's farm manager, Kale, and his wife, Molly, opened the door, Bud could see from the expressions on their faces that his day was going to soon go south, and he wondered if it had anything to do with a perfect crime.

3

Molly was the first to come in, Kale behind her, and Bud could see both looked upset. Molly was the manager of the Melon View B&B, the remodeled farmhouse on his and Wilma Jean's farm, and as she sat down across from Howie, she gave him a dirty look.

"This is all *your* doing," she said.

"Now Molly, he really didn't have anything to do with it," Kale cautioned, standing next to her, there being no more empty chairs.

"What'd I do this time?" Howie asked, now standing and looking like he was regretting staying. "I need to get to work."

"Oh, no, you don't," Molly replied. "You can just sit right back down and face the music, Mr. Mayor. If you hadn't brought all these artists here, this wouldn't be going on."

Sitting back down, Howie replied with chagrin, "I *didn't* bring any artists here. Man, this mayor thing is getting out of hand—I'm getting it from all sides. First, everyone's mad at me for something I *did* do, and now they're mad at something I *didn't* do."

"Goes with being mayor," Bud replied. "But Molly, what's going on?"

Kale answered, "The whole town's swarming with artists—some kind of event. We all just figured Howie arranged for them to come here as part of his efforts to bring more business in. The B&B's full, and we just had a to-do there. I was out in the field, so Molly took the brunt of it."

"If you didn't arrange for them to come, who did?" Molly asked Howie.

Bud replied, "Molly, nobody knows much about it yet, but it appears Howie had nothing to do with it. What happened?"

Molly replied, "Every room at the Melon View is full—10 people all told. I've never been so busy cooking and cleaning, and Wilma Jean can't come help like she usually would, as she's too busy at the cafe, so Kale's been helping. It appears there's some kind of art thing going on where people paint outdoors, then when it's all over they'll hang the paintings somewhere and have them judged and then put them up for sale. This was just from what we've been overhearing from them talking at breakfast."

"It's called plein air painting," Howie said.

Molly gave him another look, saying, "Then you *did* arrange it all, didn't you?"

"No, I just know what plein air painting is," Howie said defensively. "Everyone knows that—it's when you paint out in the plain air."

Bud, now clicking the stapler in frustration, again asked, "What happened?"

"There are these two guys, Tad and Charles, who got into a big fight," Kale offered. "I was around them a little while helping Molly serve breakfast, and you could tell they didn't care for each other. I have no idea why they're even staying in the same place. The one guy, Tad, was out all night, and when he came back just before breakfast, he was acting kind of strange. He was very unkempt looking."

"It has something to do with Charles' wife," Molly said. "But after breakfast, Kale was out in the field plowing, and these two guys came downstairs and started talking to each other. Tad was being really curt, but Charles was trying to be nice. Then Tad started yelling something about the married couple taking some artwork and not returning it, and before I could say anything, he pushed

Charles, then Charles pushed him back and he fell against the fireplace."

Molly paused, almost ready to cry, then continued.

"Some of the other guests broke it up, and Charles and his wife left. Tad, the guy who'd started the whole thing, his hand was bleeding, but he wouldn't let me help him, and he went back up to his room, then came out and left with his stuff, his hand all bandaged. I want you to come arrest him if he comes back, Bud."

"Why do you think he's coming back?" Bud asked.

Kale replied, "He's supposed to stay a week. He did have his suitcase and art stuff with him, so maybe he's not coming back, but if he does, I want him gone."

Bud shook his head, then said, "Well, maybe he left for good, but if not, call me, and I'll come out. You guys don't want to risk him attacking anyone else, if he's that kind of guy."

"I'm kind of afraid to go back to the B&B," Molly said. "What if he comes back and starts more trouble?"

"Was he behaving himself before all this?" Bud asked.

"Well, at first he seemed really nice, very considerate—but when his ex-wife showed up with her new husband yesterday, he started acting kind of sullen, then he left and was gone all night. I have no idea why he rented a room if he's going to stay out all night."

"Call me if he returns. I'll come over and ask him to leave."

"Can you do that?" Kale asked.

"Yes, since Wilma Jean and I own the place," Bud replied. "I'll refund his money and ask him to go peacefully. If he won't leave and keeps causing trouble, I can file a restraining order."

Molly stood, then asked Howie, "You really don't know anything about this art event?"

Howie, now looking somewhat official, said, "No, but as mayor, you can bet I'll find out and see what can be done about it."

Molly frowned. "It *is* nice to have the business..."

"We don't need that kind of business," Kale replied tersely. "Let's go get some groceries, then go home. I doubt very much if anyone will be coming back before evening, since they're going out in the backcountry to paint."

As Kale started out the door, Molly following, his face went white. He turned back and said, "Sheriff, here's the couple from the B&B, Charles and Kate. Charles is the one who pushed Kate's ex-husband Tad into the fireplace, injuring his hand."

Just then, a middle-aged couple came through the door, dressed in stylish hiking clothing, the man wearing a dark blue t-shirt with the words *Let it Gogh* under a picture of Van Gogh. The woman was wearing a red and yellow-striped polo-type shirt, and both wore hiking shorts and boots. They looked somewhat panicked as the man asked, "Sheriff Shumway?"

"What can I help you with?" Bud asked, noting the Van Gogh shirt and thinking of the letter he'd received the night before.

"We're here to report a body," the man said in a voice so soft Bud had to strain to hear him.

"Someone's dead?" Bud asked, trying to verify what the man had said.

"Someone's dead. A dead body," the man repeated, looking as if he might pass out. "Way out in the boonies. Out by Black Dragon Canyon."

4

"Have a seat," Bud said, offering the woman the chair Molly had just sat in. Howie stood, giving the man his chair, as Bud asked, "Could I get your names and some contact information?"

The man handed Bud a business card that indicated he was an insurance claims adjuster as the woman said quietly, "I'm Kate Meadows, and this is my husband, Charles. We're from Lake Tahoe. We're staying at their B&B." She nodded toward Molly and Kale. "We're here for the Plein Desert Air Festival."

"Can you describe where you found this person and anything you might know about them?" Bud asked.

Charles, looking as if he was slowly gathering himself, replied, "He's about a hundred feet past the petroglyph panel, on the right-hand side of the canyon."

Bud asked, "Do you know who it was?"

Kate, looking like she might start crying, said, "It's my ex-husband, Tad. He and Charles had a bit of an altercation this morning at the B&B." She looked at Molly and Kale, then added, "They saw it. But we had nothing to do with this. We all parted ways, and we went out by Black Dragon Canyon, assuming it would be a safe place for us to go paint."

Bud said, "You'll be around for a few more days, won't you? I'd like to get more information, but for now, I think it's best if I go see what's going on before anyone else comes upon the body."

"We'll be here until after the silent auction. We came a long ways for this, and it's my wife's first show, so we really don't want to leave, even though this is very traumatic."

"I understand," Bud said. "I'm going to go on out there now, but I'd like to ask you more questions later, if you don't mind. When's a good time?"

Kate replied. "We'll be back for the steak dinner, but I want to go back to the room right now for awhile. I need a cup of tea or something to help me relax. It's not every day one comes upon..."

Molly put her arm around Kate's shoulder and said, "You guys come on back, dear, and I'll make sure you get something soothing. We're going to make a quick grocery run, and then I'll make you some peppermint tea and fresh blueberry scones."

As they all stood to go, Howie asked, "Any idea what happened to the guy?"

Charles, looking concerned, said, "We saw nothing obvious on his body, though we didn't touch him, mind you. He was at the base of a big rock by the canyon wall, on his back, as if he'd fallen."

"Was he maybe shot as he was falling?" Howie asked.

Giving him a puzzled look, Charles replied, "No, not that I could tell. Are you a deputy?"

"Howie used to be sheriff here," Bud explained. "He's now our mayor."

Charles stood, saying, "He looked like he was sleeping, but he didn't respond when we asked him if he was alright. It was then that we noticed he wasn't breathing. Maybe he had a heart attack. But we need to get back to the B&B before we both collapse."

They were soon out the door, followed by Molly and Kale.

Howie sat back down, saying, "That was way too much drama. Makes me glad I'm not sheriff anymore."

"Howie, a few minutes ago you were wishing you were back in

law enforcement," Bud replied. "But don't you find it odd that they
didn't call 911 or someone for medical help after finding this guy?"

"It *is* odd," Howie replied. "They just assumed he was a goner and
came straight here, or so it seems. But they did say he wasn't breathing, and there's no cell service out in the canyon."

"But wouldn't most people do CPR or something?"

"Maybe they don't know CPR—or maybe they're mad at the guy
and were hoping he was dead, after the incident at the B&B. Or
maybe, just maybe, Sheriff, they killed him, then they made sure to
come here to report it so they'd look innocent. But are you wanting
me to go out to Black Dragon with you?"

Bud replied, "It's OK, Howie. I can handle it alone. I'll call the
ambulance folks to come help." He knew Howie had no innate
defenses against such things as body recoveries.

Howie, looking relieved, said, "I need to get over to the drive-in
and make some barbecue sauce. But you know you can call me if you
need me, Sheriff."

Bud slipped on his jacket, and they walked out the door. As he
turned to lock it, he could hear a distant droning. Looking up, he was
astounded to see a large cumbersome-looking aircraft in the near
distance, moving so slowly it looked like it was ready to crash.

"Holy cow, Sheriff!" Howie yelled. "That's an Airbus Beluga! What
in hellbells is it doing over Green River?"

"What's a Beluga? Isn't that a whale?" Bud asked.

"It's a super transporter, a wide-body plane made for carrying
outsized cargo, the next iteration after the Super Guppy. They call it
the Beluga because it resembles a whale, though the front of it looks
more like a porpoise to me. It's made in Europe. I don't think there
are more than a half-dozen on the entire planet."

As they stood watching, the plane's nose lifted upward and it
began gaining altitude, then it suddenly dipped and headed straight
for the ground.

"I can't watch," Howie said. "It's going to crash! Bud, it looks like
it's right over the elementary school!"

They stood transfixed, watching as the plane did a barrel roll, then, regaining altitude, disappeared into the distance until it was a white dot toward the cliffs of the Blue Castle, fading away.

Howie, shaking his head, said, "It's a good thing it's commercial and not a passenger plane. Can you imagine how passengers would feel after a stunt like that? I hope they didn't destroy their cargo."

Bud, still not believing his eyes, replied, "Howie, was that for real? How could you do a barrel roll in a huge plane like that and not crash?"

"Ask Tex Johnston," Howie replied. "He's the pilot who did a barrel roll in a Boeing 707 prototype over Lake Washington in 1955. He said you can do a barrel roll safely in any kind of plane as long as you keep it at a positive G so the plane's oil and fluids don't leak."

Bud replied, "But Howie, something didn't seem quite right about it."

"Agreed. It's definitely not right to pull a stunt like that over a town."

"It's like it wasn't as far away as it looked or something, and the sound wasn't right."

"It does seem kind of odd, Sheriff," Howie said. "Did you know that in 1999, a Beluga carried a large painting from the Louvre to Tokyo? The canvas was about 10 by 12 feet and too big to fit into a Boeing 747. They transported it in a special pressurized container."

"No kidding?" Bud replied, wondering how Howie's brain could hold so much trivia.

Howie continued, "Good thing the pilot didn't do any barrel rolls. But Sheriff, I've decided to do a ride-along, if it's OK with you. Let's go on out to Black Dragon and see what happened. I have a feeling you're going to need my help, especially if we get a report of a crashed Beluga."

Bud shook his head as they got into the Emery County Sheriff's Land Cruiser, drove through town, turned onto the freeway, and headed west.

5

Bud and Howie rode along for awhile in silence, the barren emptiness of the surrounding gray Mancos shales mirroring their dread at having to go retrieve a body.

As they finally crested the long rise of the Oyster Shell Reef and dropped down into the more colorful red layers of the Summerville Formation, Bud asked, "Was that Beluga going 1G? How could one tell?"

"It must've been," Howie replied. "Or it would've crashed. When Tex Johnston did that barrel roll, he flew back over and did it again because he didn't think anyone would believe their eyes after the first one. He said later that it was perfectly safe, and an airplane doesn't recognize altitude, as long as you stay at 1G—it never knows it's inverted."

"I kind of remember something from school about mass and velocity being related—if you speed up, does your mass decrease?" Bud asked. "Maybe if I moved faster I could lose a little weight."

"Something like that, Sheriff," Howie replied pensively, and Bud could tell he was distracted by the upcoming body recovery. "But Bud, mass and weight aren't the same thing. Mass is the amount of matter you have, while weight is a measure of how the force of gravity acts upon that mass. Mass is a constant, but weight equals mass times gravity."

"So, if there's no gravity, I wouldn't weigh anything? Is that why astronauts float in space, there's no gravity?"

Howie replied, "Yes, but you don't need to go into outer space if you want to lose weight, just go up in a plane. You're farther from the earth's gravity. But Sheriff, we need to think about this guy we're going to retrieve, not physics. How are we going to get him back?"

"We're just going to check it out, Howie. If there actually is a body, we'll call the ambulance crew to come get it."

"Why wouldn't there be a body?"

"Maybe the guy wasn't really dead and left. You never know."

They soon crossed the San Rafael River, a wide band of tamarisk shrubs marking the actual riverway. Layered cliffs soon pushed the freeway into a narrow valley, which eventually opened up with views of the formidable San Rafael Reef ahead, its tall sandstone ramparts seeming to block forward progress.

Bud said, "Howie, I still find it odd that the couple didn't contact me as soon as they got out of Black Dragon, but instead drove all the way into town to my office. There's cell service as soon as you get out of the canyon."

"Maybe they didn't know that," Howie replied. "It's not really that odd, Sheriff. They don't know the country, and maybe they didn't know your number."

"And they apparently didn't even do anything to verify he was dead," Bud added. "It sounds like they just stood there looking at him, noticed he didn't seem to be breathing, then left. I mean, what if he'd fallen and just had the wind knocked out of him?"

"I don't think most people are very thorough when it comes to medical stuff, Bud," Howie said. "Especially if they think someone's dead. I mean, I have to admit that I myself am kind of squeamish..." His voice trailed off.

Now slowing as he searched through his pockets with one hand, Bud replied, "I think I lost my harmonica."

"The one you found in the school yard?" Howie asked. "If so, you're sunk, Sheriff. What are you going to use to fiddle with to help you think? And it looks like with all that's going on, you're going to need to do some heavy-duty thinking—and fiddling. But the gate's coming up."

Bud slowed even more and turned onto the freeway's shoulder, driving down the bank to a closed gate in a sagging wire fence. Howie jumped out and opened it as Bud drove through, then closed the gate behind them, jumping back in.

They were at the foot of the Reef, and even though there was no signage or indications of where the road went, it looked well-used, a two-track with patches of sand here and there heading back toward huge sandstone walls.

Bud deftly crossed a sandy wash, gunning the Land Cruiser on through, saying, "This is the wash that drains Petroglyph and Double Arch canyons. You've been out here before, haven't you?"

Howie replied that he hadn't.

"They're small canyons between Black Dragon and the freeway. Petroglyph Canyon has a few petroglyphs of bighorn sheep and some human-like figures. It's pretty short. Double Arch Canyon splits off from it and dead-ends in about a mile at a deep pothole with a spectacular arch on the skyline called Spirit Arch. It used to be called Double Arch but some guide book writer renamed it. I kind of prefer the old name."

They could see a dark gray sedan parked under a few scraggly-looking cottonwoods that drank from the wash when it rained.

"Must be someone hiking," Bud remarked. "It's not far back in there."

"Nevada plates. Must be tourists," Howie replied. "A car like that wouldn't be able to go any farther anyway without high-clearance."

They continued until a rough road split off from the two-track, going directly into the maw of the Reef, following Black Dragon Wash, one of the few seasonal waterways that cut all the way through the huge sandstone uplift.

Bud knew an old wagon road once followed the wash, the only passage through the Reef until the freeway was blasted through

Spotted Wolf Canyon to the south. The new passage through Spotted Wolf was an engineering marvel of its time, for the original wash had been a mere 20 feet wide through sheer sandstone walls.

Just before the road continued into the depths of Black Dragon Canyon, they came upon a parked vehicle.

"That looks like Ted Henderson's old truck," Howie said, nodding toward an old Ford F100 painted a deep navy blue. "It has to be, as he did the paint job himself. It's one of a kind."

They stopped and got out, examining the truck. Looking through the side window, they could see an old straw hat, a Stanley thermos, a box of Ritz crackers, and what looked like an empty aluminum case with the words, *DJI Mavic*, its lid open. Next to all that was a pillow and a green Coleman sleeping bag.

"You don't suppose he's in here hiking?" Bud asked.

"Could be," Howie said. "And I sure hope he's not the body they found. He's a really nice guy. He's the one who did the portrait of me and Maureen and little Malcolm that's on our living-room wall."

Bud replied, "He did one of me and Wilma Jean for our anniversary. He and I have had some good photography discussions. He's the one who taught me how to shoot sunstars. Hopefully he's just up the canyon taking pictures," Bud replied. "But she said the guy was her ex-husband, and Ted's never been divorced, as far as I know."

Howie replied, "I bet he has his drone out here, judging from that case. But let's get going."

They were soon in the depths of Black Dragon Canyon, its huge Navajo Sandstone walls closing in on them as the two-track became more difficult, squeezed by rock ledges and sand pits. Bud drove slowly on until they finally reached a place where the canyon widened.

It was the end of the road, such that it was, the wash now blocked by fallen trees and rocks, the old wagon trail long unusable. Bud had himself once hiked all the way through the canyon, coming out far beneath the freeway where he could see people looking down from a pullout high on the flanks of the Swell.

"Looks like we're here," Howie said as Bud stopped across from a spectacular wall draped with desert varnish, a wooden rail fence in front. "Is this where the Black Dragon is?"

"It is," Bud replied, "Though I've never figured out how they made a dragon out of it. It looks more like a strange bird with outspread wings, and it's not black, it's red."

They could see petroglyphs on the canyon wall, and a huge pile of rubble and talus beyond the panel ended in an alcove, its black depths uninviting.

They walked to the wooden fence where they could make out several elongated human and animal images.

"These look like Barrier Canyon style, which is really old," Bud said. "Like thousands of years. And these figures next to them are Fremont, who were contemporary with the Anasazi, or Ancient ones, as they now call them. The ones chiseled into the rock are petroglyphs, and the painted ones are pictographs. And over here's the supposed dragon."

"What did they paint with?" Howie asked, looking up in awe at strange robed figures almost as tall as he was.

"Red ochre, though other panels have different colors. They also used charcoal, plant dyes, that kind of thing," Bud replied, craning his neck to see the tall figures.

"You seem to know a lot about them," Howie added.

Bud replied, "Not really. Everyone in this country knows the basics if they've been out in the canyons at all. There's lots of what we call rock art all over these canyons. Eldon and Frosty know where a lot of it is. Eldon told me that at one point someone chalked over several figures, combining them into what appeared to be a dragonlike image, which gave the canyon its name. I don't know if that's true or not, but this one image here, the one that looks like a strange bird, is what they call the Black Dragon."

"Why would they chalk over them?"

"To take photos, I guess," Bud replied. "It's now illegal, though it didn't used to be. People do all kinds of destructive things, even use rock art for target practice."

They stood in silence for a moment, then Bud said, "Howie, we need to get on with it. I feel like you do—it's never much fun doing a body recovery, but it has to be done."

"How much farther did they say it was to where they found the guy? About a quarter mile?" Howie asked.

"No, they said about a hundred feet, so he should be about over at the base of the rubble below that alcove."

"But didn't they say it looked like he'd fallen? How could he fall off that? It's a slope, not a cliff."

"I don't know, Howie. Maybe he was up at the alcove and rolled down and hit his head on a rock or something. But let's go see what we can find."

As they turned to go, Bud noted a series of small round holes poked into the nearby sand. He bent to examine them as Howie picked up a small black object, saying, "Looks like a flashlight, Sheriff."

Taking the flashlight, Bud could see it was rectangular, about six inches long, black with a red lens, and bore the words, *Celestron Night Vision LED Flashlight Made in China.*

"That's odd," Bud replied, clicking it on and shining the red beam on the leg of his tan khaki pants. "Howie, this is a photography night light. It uses red light to preserve your night vision. It's rectangular so you can set it on a surface and it won't roll. And these holes must be from a tripod. It looks like someone's been out here taking photos, and I bet that someone was our photographer friend, Ted Henderson. It's very possible he was planning on staying out late tonight for some more shots, and thus the flashlight."

"He may be staying out here forever if we can't find his body, Bud, assuming it's him. Let's get going and get this over with."

With that, they turned and began trudging on up the canyon.

6

"Do you suppose someone committed the perfect crime?" Howie asked. "It doesn't look to me like there's a body around here, Sheriff."

They were searching near the canyon wall, but so far had found nothing.

"Howie, be quiet for a minute," Bud said, grabbing Howie's arm.

"I thought I heard it too," Howie whispered. "Sounds like someone talking, maybe back where you come into the canyon."

"Probably some tourists," Bud replied. "There never used to be anyone out here, but Green River's trying to promote it as a scenic attraction, along with Crystal Geyser. Let's keep walking upcanyon and see what we can find. Maybe the couple who found the body underestimated the distance."

They continued walking along and were soon at the rubble slope below the alcove.

"Sheriff, look up by that bush in front of the alcove. What do you think that black thing could be?"

Bud looked up to where Howie pointed, then said, "It looks like a case of some kind. Maybe we should go take a look."

It took some doing, but they eventually climbed to the alcove's entrance, huffing and puffing, where Howie picked up what indeed was a case.

"It's a camera case, Bud. This is kind of like playing that game *Clue*, where you keep finding stuff."

"It reminds me more of Hansel and Gretel, Howie, except instead of breadcrumbs, we're following camera gear."

Bud looked inside the case, but it was empty. A plastic ID tag on the strap read, *Ted Henderson*, along with his phone number.

Finally catching their breath, they eyed the entrance to the alcove, which had been reduced to a small narrow slot from the rockfall.

"It's a tight fit in there, Howie," Bud said. "But it might be a good idea to search it. If Ted came up here, he may be inside."

"Why would he want to go in there?" Howie asked. "I think I could fit in there, but I'm not sure I want to. I mean..."

"It's OK, Howie. Let's just shine a light in and see what we can see. Ted probably just climbed up here to take some photos and inadvertently dropped his case. He's kind of a big guy, so I doubt if he could fit in there anyway."

Now on his knees, Bud shone the Celestron light through the narrow entrance, trying to see inside. He finally got onto his stomach, sticking his head inside, trying to acclimate his vision to the inky darkness.

"Some people call this Black Dragon Cave," he said, shining the light all around. "And I think there's something in here."

With that, he squeezed on his stomach through the slot, then pulled himself up onto his knees. Looking around, he said, "Howie, see if you can get in here. I think I'm going to need your help."

Howie was soon inside next to Bud, and Bud shone the light directly on what looked to be someone sleeping, face up, a camera by his side.

"That sure looks like Ted Henderson," Howie said. "Can we stand up in here?"

Bud shone the light upwards, then pulled himself onto his feet.

"This is actually a big alcove, it's just that the entrance is almost closed off by rubble. Look up, Howie. See how black the ceiling is? Someone's had a fire in here and used it for shelter."

Howie bent over and picked something up, holding it in Bud's light. "That someone was probably native people from long ago," Howie said. "This looks like an ancient hide scraper."

They walked over to Ted's body, shining the light down on his face.

"He looks like he's sleeping, Bud," Howie said. "Are we sure he's actually dead?"

Bud picked up Ted's arm, feeling for a pulse in his wrist.

"He's as cold as ice, Howie. He's definitely deceased. We're going to need help getting him out of here. Why don't you go back to the Cruiser and get out to where you have a signal and call the ambulance and coroner? I'll stay here and look around, see if I can find anything that would give us an idea why he died."

Howie, sounding relieved, said, "It's sure spooky in here, Sheriff. Are you sure you don't want to just come with me? He's not going anywhere."

"It's OK, Howie," Bud replied. "I really need to stay here and look around. Just come on back after you get ahold of them. Bring that thermos with you."

"Roger," Howie replied, sliding out through the opening. Bud could hear him say something else, but it was muffled, and Howie was soon gone.

Turning back to the body, Bud shone the light all around, looking for clues. Finding nothing, he picked up the camera. It was a somewhat expensive-looking Nikon, which didn't surprise him, as he knew Ted had started his own wedding and portrait photography business after retiring from the local gas company. He'd done quite well, branching out to the nearby towns of Radium and Price, as Green River itself didn't have much business.

Bud noted the camera was dented and covered with sand. He knew Ted took good care of his equipment—had he dropped it when he died? Surprised that it would still turn on, he quickly scanned through photos of the canyon, the petroglyphs, a few wildflowers, and some night skies with stars. He noted it had a filter on its front.

Turning the camera back off, he put it back in its case, which Howie had brought into the alcove with him. Bud next picked up a tripod near Ted's body, noting it was an expensive brand.

He now began the more unsightly task of searching the body, beginning with Ted's pockets, where he found his billfold and a folded note. Shining the light on it, it read, *F-2.8, ISO 1600, 20 seconds. Focus on Polaris and tape it.*

He recognized it as being a note for night-sky photography, which, along with the star shots, showed that Ted had stayed out in the canyon after dark. He placed the note in his pocket, then began searching all around the alcove, but found nothing.

Sitting on a big rock at the edge of the alcove, light off, Bud now realized Ted's drone was nowhere nearby, and he wondered what had happened to it. He then thought back to what the couple had said when they'd come into his office.

Hadn't Charles said that Ted's body was at the base of the canyon wall, on his back, as if he'd fallen off a rock? It seemed like things weren't matching up like they should—there was no way he could've fallen while in the alcove, as there was nothing to fall from. Maybe he'd tripped and hit his head or something, but there really wasn't much of anything to hit it on, Bud mused, the floor of the alcove being soft sand.

He got up and started pacing back and forth in the dark. Reaching for his harmonica, he remembered it was missing, so he picked up the scraper Howie had found and began fiddling with it, trying to think.

Had someone moved the body, hoping to hide it, after the couple had found it? If so, why? Had someone murdered Ted, hid when the couple came by, then somehow dragged the body up the steep slope and into the alcove, which would be no easy task? Or had they killed him after he was already in the alcove? Did the couple, Charles and Kate, have anything to do with Ted's death?

And why would anyone want to kill the gentle giant of a photographer who was popular around Green River, always laughing and smiling and making people feel good? He didn't seem like the kind of guy who would have any enemies, especially the kind who would want him dead. Had he witnessed something he shouldn't have? And if he'd been killed, it seemed likely that the killer would want his expensive camera and tripod, instead of leaving them in the sand.

Bud would go through the photos in more detail back at his office, but it seemed to him that Ted had died of natural causes, seeing there were no marks on his body that he could make out.

He was now regretting not going with Howie, as he was craving a cup of coffee, and he knew it would be awhile before Howie could drive out of the canyon to make the call and then come back. He pulled a granola bar from his pocket and started to open it, then decided it would be more palatable sitting outside in the sun, not next to a body. Besides, he was getting tired of the darkness—it was making him feel desultory.

He went back to the entrance, carrying the tripod and the camera case, and began to crawl back through the opening, now feeling claustrophobic and a bit panicky.

As he slipped through, he could feel something scratching along his stomach. Thinking it was maybe a scorpion, he quickly slid out, then turned and shone his light back to see what it was.

Surprised, he picked it up—it was a gold ring, and on its face were the words, *Firmum in vita nihil*—the exact same words as on the seal of the letter he'd received the previous evening—*Nothing in life is permanent*.

7

Bud sat in his office, intently studying a photo of a Datura flower on his computer screen. The photo was nicely done, the plant's large white blossoms wide open in the evening twilight, a dark hawkmoth with splashes of pink on its stout body, hovering as it fed on the sweet nectar from the plant with its long tongue.

Still tired from the previous day, Bud got himself another cup of coffee from the pot on the small table by his file cabinet, then sat back down. He groaned, his legs a bit sore from climbing the steep slope up to Black Dragon Cave. It had also been a chore carrying Ted Henderson's body back down the slope, even though the EMTs and Howie had helped, Howie also driving Ted's pickup back after they'd found the keys in Ted's pocket.

Once back at the office and ready to go home, it had turned out to be an even longer day than usual, as there had been a break-in at Jay's Tavern that Bud had to investigate, though all that was stolen was Jay's supply of steaks.

Sipping the hot coffee and wishing he had a dollop of vanilla-bean ice cream to put in it, Bud looked down at the front of his shirt where two wide suspenders were attached to his khaki pants. The suspenders were a nice blue color, and he had the sudden urge to snap them, but he knew it was probably a bad idea with nothing between them and his skin but his denim shirt, which was almost the same color as the suspenders.

He groaned again, but this time not from his sore muscles, but rather from the memory of opening the package he'd found on the kitchen table that morning, kind of wishing he'd pretended not to notice.

It was from his wife and had a note with it that read:

Hon, saw these at Wiggins Diggins up in Price today and thought of you. I know you'll find them handy. XXXOOO Wilma Jean

He'd wondered what could possibly be in the slim package, hoping for maybe some Peppermint Life Savers or even some jerky. But coming from Wiggins Diggins, he knew it had to be something used, as it was a second-hand store, and as far as he knew they didn't sell candy.

Opening the package, he'd felt a bit disappointed, but no matter, as it was the thought that counted, he mused, even though he knew the gift held a message.

That not-so-subtle message was that he was getting enough of a paunch to need something to help hold up his pants. He thought of his Uncle Junior, who always wore red-white-and-blue-striped American flag suspenders to hold up his worn Wrangler jeans, his stomach hanging over enough that he could actually tuck his pants up under it. Bud grimaced, worried that it might run in the family.

He knew he needed to slow down on things like ice cream and apple pie, but how in hellsbells was a man supposed to exercise self-restraint when his wife owned a cafe and always brought home delicious left-overs? It seemed like an impossible situation, though he knew his love of ice cream was part of the problem.

At least the suspenders kind of blended in with his shirt, so maybe nobody would notice them, he hoped, but he wondered who *GW* was, his initials embroidered on the front of each suspender. He shrugged his shoulders, turning his attention back to the photo on his computer screen.

Such a photo would be hard to take, Bud thought, for the contrast between the light creamy Datura flowers and the dark moth made for a high dynamic range, and the fading evening light would make getting the right exposure tricky.

Bud was pretty sure that Ted had spent the night out in the canyon, as he'd also downloaded a number of beautiful night-sky photos showing a sky full of stars framed by black canyon walls, which went with the note he'd found in Ted's pocket about camera settings. He also had a number of photos of a stand of Fremont cottonwoods in their spring-green coats, and some of the canyon walls with white clouds streaming by in the sky. The time stamp on them all said they'd been taken before he'd died.

He opened a new computer window and did an Internet search on *hawkmoth*.

Hawk or sphinx moths are nocturnal pollinators, and like butterflies, are covered with tiny scales, the dust you see on your fingers when you try to catch one. These magnificent animals have long narrow wings and thick bodies. They are fast flyers and are highly aerobatic, and many species can hover in place. Some can even briefly fly backwards or dart away.

Hawkmoths are experts at finding sweet-smelling flowers after dark. They are especially fond of Datura (also called moonflower and Jimson weed), Mirabilis (Four O'Clock) and Queen-of-the-Night cactus blossoms.

They have the longest tongues (some up to 14 inches long) of any other moth or butterfly. Moths pick up pollen on their legs and wings when they visit flowers and deposit pollen on subsequent floral visits.

Bud paused. A moth with a tongue over a foot long? It seemed impossible. He now keyed in *Datura*:

Datura is a showy plant with large, white (sometimes tinged purple), funnel-shaped flowers that bloom in the late afternoon and evening and close in the morning.

Datura flowers are pollinated at night by hawkmoths. The flowers are highly fragrant with long floral tubes concealing pools of thin but abundant nectar. The moths hover like hummingbirds and unfurl a very long proboscis to get the nectar.

Datura leaves are large, dark green grayish, and velvety. They can cause dermatitis to those with sensitive skin. The flowers are 6 to 7 inches long and 5 inches wide. All parts of this plant are poisonous, containing toxic alkaloids. Livestock and people have been fatally poisoned by ingesting the plant and seeds.

Coffee gone, Bud leaned back in his chair. He'd downloaded the photos from Ted Henderson's camera and studied each one several times, but something was bothering him, something he couldn't quite put his finger on.

He again brought up a photo of Black Dragon Canyon, admiring the way Ted had captured the sunset glow on the smooth walls. Slowly scanning through the photos again, Bud stopped on the one of the clouds above the canyon—something seemed odd and out of place, but he couldn't quite figure out what it was.

From the way the clouds stretched out like long streamers, it looked to be a long exposure, but something was wrong with it—he slowly enlarged the image until it dawned on him that a small part of the canyon wall looked odd. Zooming in closer, he could see an unnatural yellow and red stripe, though blurred, but it definitely didn't blend into the rest of the scene. Next to it was another blur, though this one was a dark blue. The colors were smeared to the point that it was hard to even make them out.

He zoomed back out and sat there, trying to figure out what was going on. Everything was in perfect focus except for the colored smudges along the base of the wall, which were blurred beyond recognition and almost looked ghost-like.

He knew he'd taken photos himself that had strange aberrations in them, and he knew it was always caused by light reflecting through the lens elements. He decided that this photo probably had the same effect.

He then decided he needed to get busy instead of going down some rabbit hole. It was time to go out to the Melon View B&B to see if he could clear up some things that were bothering him, mostly the odd fact that Ted was renting a room at a local B&B when he had a house nearby in town.

He and Howie had discussed this, and they'd finally decided that maybe he was having work done on his house or something. It seemed strange, but not unheard of. And why had he gotten into an argument with Charles?

Picking up the phone, Bud dialed the B&B. Molly answered, and he asked, "Molly, is this a good time for me to come out and check through Ted's room? I need to do a thorough look to be sure there's no evidence there."

Molly replied, "Oh my gosh, Bud! I had no idea you would be needing to go through the room. I already cleaned it and rented it out. We're totally inundated with people looking for a place to stay. I had it rented before the day was even out. I'm so sorry."

Bud replied, "Well, Molly, I know how thorough you are, so maybe you saved me some time. Did you find anything of interest?"

"No, nothing. It looks like he took everything with him when he went out for the day, as he didn't even leave any clothes. I found that odd, but after thinking about the fight the two got into that morning, I think he'd decided to not stay. Kate and Charles told me there was no way he'd be coming back—after all, they saw his body, you know."

Bud wasn't sure what to say. Finally, he replied, "Well, I guess you did what you thought was best. I doubt if there was anything there that would've helped anyway."

"Oh, Bud, I always tidy up the rooms for people, even if they're staying. I give them fresh towels and make the beds and all that. I've even started putting a mint on each pillow, kind of a special touch. But when I saw he hadn't left a thing, I went ahead and changed the sheets and got it ready for the next person, just in case. That evening, I rented it out."

"It's OK," Bud replied. "Like I said, you probably saved me some time. Everything else going OK?"

"Other than being swamped, it's fine," Molly replied. "I'll be glad when it's all over. These artists have totally taken the place over. They even set up an easel with a big empty canvas on it in the common room. The idea is for everyone to add some element as time goes on, making it a communal work, then they'll auction it off at the end of the festival. It'll be interesting to see what they come up with."

"I'm going to stop by," Bud said. "Thanks, Molly, and let me know if you see or hear anything of interest."

They hung up, Bud wondering if Ted had taken his stuff back home, then gone out to the canyon. He still found it odd that a photographer would want to rent a room in a busy B&B with a bunch of plein air artists, especially when he had a perfectly good home in town.

He shrugged. He would go by Ted's house to check things out, as he had the address from his driver's license. He needed to notify Ted's next of kin as soon as he could figure out who they were. He wouldn't know for sure what the cause of death was until he heard back from the coroner.

He absent-mindedly snapped his suspenders, winced, put on his jacket and headed out the door, again wondering where he'd left his harmonica.

8

Bud hadn't been to the Melon View B&B for some time, maybe even since he'd helped Wilma Jean clean it and move in some new furniture when they'd first opened it up, though Molly and Kale had done most of the work.

He'd forgotten how nice it was, a restored farmhouse with its old winding oak staircase and stained-glass window in the foyer. And it looked like Molly and Kale had been doing some serious gardening, making the big grassy lawn look like a park with flagstone walks and benches under the big willows, as well as numerous flowerbeds, wind chimes, and hummingbird feeders.

He paused, wondering why he didn't feel particularly attached to the place, not like someone who was a co-owner should. He felt like it was more Wilma Jean's deal, it being her idea to turn it into a B&B. He was more interested in the big fields and the quonset hut on the other side of the farm where they kept the equipment and he helped Kale when he had time.

Going on inside, he could see several people sitting in the big living room, drinking tea and snacking on trays of cookies, pastries, and finger sandwiches.

"Bud! You're just in time for tea," Molly said. "Or would you prefer some coffee?"

Bud replied, "I'll have a cup of coffee, Molly, thanks. But no goodies. I don't want to ruin my appetite for dinner."

Molly smiled, then brought him a cup of coffee from the kitchen along with a slice of pound cake. Bud thanked her, suspecting that she knew there probably wasn't much that could ruin his appetite.

"I like your new suspenders," Molly smiled. "But who's GW? Wilma Jean's making you wear them, isn't she? But are you looking for Charles and Kate? I think they're still out painting."

"Did they recover from finding Ted's body?"

"Yes, they seemed fine. A lot better than I would be, that's for sure."

"Molly I'd like to ask you a few questions, if you don't mind. First, what kind of vehicle was Ted driving?"

"He had a gray sedan of some type. I didn't really pay much attention, with everyone coming and going, and most everyone drives a gray sedan these days. But look, here comes the fellow that took Tad's room. Hello Mr. Papillon. Go on over and have some tea and cookies."

Bud smiled and said hello as a thin man came inside, nodded at them, then immediately helped himself to tea and cookies, going on upstairs to his room. Bud couldn't help but note how much the guy reminded him of Groucho Marx with his thick eyebrows and mustache, as well as his dark suit jacket and pants.

His black hair stuck out from under a black fedora with a white silk headband, and he wore a thick cream-colored scarf wrapped around his neck that looked to Bud more like a turban that had accidentally slipped down. Oddly enough, he also wore black leather driving gloves, even though it wasn't cold.

As soon as the guy was gone, Molly whispered, "Good lord, what a handsome man. Be still my heart that only beats a few times a week."

Bud laughed as Molly continued. "You know I'm being sarcastic, of course. He kind of gives me the creeps—he's a weird duck. His eyebrows and mustache look like they're made out of cardboard or something—or maybe painted on with a black marker—and he never says anything. He did manage to tell me he has a rare skin condition where he can't be in the sun at all."

"Is he an artist?"

"No. When he checked in, he said he was just here to enjoy the scenery. But he looks more like he belongs in an Edgar Allan Poe play. And he told me not to expect him for breakfast—he said it in a tone like we'd be disappointed or something, like he's famous. He seems very eccentric."

"Well, he'll fit into Green River," Bud replied, not sure what to say. "I bet you meet some interesting people here."

"Oh, I do," Molly replied. "But take a look at this."

She led Bud over near the big white brick fireplace where a large canvas stood on an easel. Someone had painted a few puffy clouds where the sky should be.

"This is the canvas I told you about. Everyone's supposed to add to it as time progresses. It'll go up for auction at the end of the festival."

"Looks like someone has a good start," Bud said.

Molly replied, "You know Bud, that guy who got in the fight with Charles wasn't very honest. He stole a whole set of our nice towels. I'd be going after him if he wasn't already dead."

"Good thing he is," Bud said. "I'd hate to think of what you might do to him."

Molly laughed. "I guess that's what they call dark humor, huh? But I need to get busy. We don't usually offer dinner, but they talked me into it. They're providing the steaks. I need to make a salad and some dessert."

"Steaks?" Bud asked, thinking of the theft at Jay's Tavern. "Who's bringing the steaks?"

"I don't know for sure," Molly replied.

"Molly, it may just be a coincidence, but someone broke into Jay's last night and took a bunch of steaks."

"That would be too weird, Bud," Molly said. "Why would

someone here steal steaks? All these people seem pretty well-heeled —heck, you have to be to stay here in the first place, as it's not cheap. And a lot of them are vegetarians, at least I think so from the way they always turn down bacon and sausage for breakfast."

"Molly, can I see the guest register? I want to check out this new guy."

Molly handed Bud the register from a nearby table.

"It says *Hawk Papillon, Sego, Utah, Social Entrepreneur.* What's a social entrepreneur?" Bud asked. "And Sego? That's a ghost town, Molly."

"I think it's all strange, Bud," Molly replied. "And I also think Hawk's a strange name. Kind of fits him, I guess. Maybe he's actually a ghost and has to stay bundled up to be visible."

"Well, I need to go," Bud replied. "But Molly, feel free to call me if anything seems amiss, even something you might consider minor."

As he turned to go, Bud saw a note propped against a flower vase on the entrance table. It read:

> Green River Gopher
> No task or errand too small.
> Joey 564-3427

"Who's this, Molly?" Bud asked.

"Oh, that's just Joey Andrews. His parents left here a month or so ago to move to Nebraska, and he stayed behind with his aunt wanting to finish high school here. He's trying to make some spending money. He helps me around here occasionally. He does good work, so I let him put that out in case guests need something. But I need to get busy."

Bud said goodbye and headed out the door, an unsettled feeling of confusion following like a cloud of dust on a farm road.

9

Bud sat under a big cottonwood tree by the softly gurgling irrigation ditch, his dogs Hoppie, Pierre, and Lindie lazily begging nearby, hoping for a bite of his grilled cheese sandwich.

It was a beautiful bluebird sky day, the fresh-green leaves of the big tree now fully unrolled and ready for a refreshing chlorophyll breakfast after the long winter.

He'd stopped by Howie's Drive-In on his way back from the Melon View, getting a grilled cheese instead of a cheeseburger, thinking of Wilma Jean's recent reminder that he needed to keep an eye on his cholesterol.

He had no idea if it was high or low, not really inclined to worry about such things as long as he felt good, but maybe she was right and he should try to eat better, something his new suspenders reminded him of every day now.

Taking a sip from his thermos of hot coffee, Bud mused on how this was possibly his favorite spot in the whole world, though now that he was thinking of it, there were a number of spots in the Big Empty that were a close second.

The beauty of this particular spot was that it was on the farm that he and Wilma Jean owned, even though they still had plenty of payments to make to Professor Krider, who'd sold them the place on time payments. But being private land, he didn't have to worry about anyone coming along and disturbing his peace.

As he divided what was left of the sandwich between the dogs, his cell phone rang.

"Yell-ow," he answered.

"Sheriff, where are you?"

It was Howie.

Bud replied, "I'm out at the farm, Sheriff."

Howie was silent for moment, then said, "Bud, hows come you're calling me sheriff? I'm not sheriff anymore."

Bud grinned. "It's in honor of you once being sheriff, Sheriff."

Howie groaned. "This is about me calling you sheriff all the time, even after you quit, right, Sheriff—I mean Bud?"

"Howie, it's OK to call me sheriff now since I'm sheriff again. But I've been wondering—do you prefer I call you Mayor or Sheriff?"

"Bud," Howie moaned. "You're making me forget why I called. I have an 11-78 to report. This is serious business."

"An 11-78? You mean an aircraft accident?"

"Yes, Sheriff, and it looks bad. I figured out what was going on with that Beluga we saw the other day. They're having an air show out here at the airport. I need to get people to keep me in the loop on what's going on around here. First, these plein air artists, and now an air show."

"Howie, if there's an 11-78, don't you think I should get on the horn to the ambulance team instead of us talking?"

"Not yet, Bud. I think you should just come on out here first. Nobody was hurt. But you need to check it out, unless you have something more important going on. Run over to Howie's and pick me up a chili-cheese dog and a root beer on your way. I already called it in, so it should be ready when you get there. Get yourself something, too, on the house."

"Roger, Sheriff," Bud replied. "But I just finished a sandwich. I need to drop the dogs off, then I'll get your hotdog and come on out. You're sure we don't need an ambulance? Did anyone call the FAA?"

"Just come on out, Sheriff," Howie replied to the sound of an airplane in the background.

Bud loaded the dogs up and headed for the bungalow, where he quickly gave them each a couple of Barkie Biscuits out in the shady yard. He then swung by Howie's Drive-In, picking up Howie's order, and was soon heading toward the airport, wondering why Howie had been so casual about an airplane crash.

As he got near the hanger, he could see a number of parked cars and a small crowd standing by the runway. Getting out of the Cruiser, he ducked as the sound of several planes came over his shoulder, and he looked up just in time to see a trio of what looked to be vintage fighter planes flying in formation.

Each had a yellow snout and blue bodies painted with white stars and stripes. Bud wasn't much of an aircraft kind of guy, but he recognized them as P-51 Mustangs, having seen an old documentary about WWII.

As he watched in fascination, the planes made a long turn over the airport, still in formation, then came back above the crowd as people took photos and clapped. But something was wrong, for the lead plane now looked like it was starting to shimmy.

Bud stood watching, fascinated, as the plane slowly began rotating and turning sideways, and it was only a matter of seconds before the following two planes crashed directly into it. The sound of metal and wood crunching was followed by debris flying from the sky as the crowd ducked and ran, trying not to get hit.

Once the debris had hit the ground, the crowd began cheering and clapping as if it had been great entertainment. Bud knew he'd been watching radio-controlled replicas, not real full-sized Mustangs. Unlike the Beluga Airbus he and Howie had seen earlier, where there had been nothing in the sky to compare the plane to, it was easy to see these were models, especially once the debris hit the ground.

Just then, he heard a voice behind him as someone put their hand on his shoulder.

"Their winderbuster busted, Bud. Let us give a moment of silence to the souls of those brave pilots."

Bud turned, grinning. It was his old friend Doc Richardson, who had once been the coroner up in Price and had married their friend Millie after she'd sold the Ghost Rock Cafe up on the Swell. The pair now lived over in Palisade, Colorado, and Bud hadn't seen them for some time.

Bud replied, "You know, nobody ever thinks of the little people in the cockpits, do they, Doc? But amazing as it sounds, the actual pilots all walked away—in fact, they're over there picking up the pieces as we speak."

"Radio-controlled aircraft can be an expensive hobby, Bud. Much more so than model railroading—by the way, do you suppose Corky's still waiting for us to connect our rail line with his way up there in Montana?"

Bud laughed, thinking of the fun they'd had on vacation with their friend Corky's model railroad setup. He asked, "Are you getting into RC stuff, Doc? What brings you over this way? Is Millie with you?"

"She's hanging out helping your wife at the cafe. Looks like we arrived in the middle of something big. The whole town's full of tourists."

Bud replied, "I guess there's this RC show here, and there's also an artists' gathering, but I'm not sure what else is going on. Are you guys staying awhile?"

"We were, but there's no place to stay," Doc replied, nodding his head in greeting as Howie walked over. "Everything's booked up."

"You can stay in our Airstream behind the house, Doc. Wilma Jean has it all glamped up. We'd sure like to spend some time with you."

Bud handed Howie his hotdog and root beer as Howie said, "Sheriff, glad you made it. Hello Doc, long time no see. Did you guys see the carnage just now? Man, I think some of these guys have more money than piloting skills."

Doc replied, "I think the worst part of flying model airplanes must be having to pick up all the pieces of the plane you've spent 80-plus hours creating. It's kind of a walk of shame."

Howie laughed, saying, "I guess any crash landing you can walk away with your aircraft under your arm is a good landing."

Bud asked, "Howie, what about that II-78 aircraft accident you called me about? Or did you anticipate the Mustangs crashing?"

Howie laughed. "I'm not psychic, Sheriff. The II-78 is over there in the brush. It's that model Airbus A300, the Beluga we saw back in town doing barrel-rolls. I watched it go down, and it reminded me of you. I thought you might enjoy the airshow."

"Thanks," Bud replied. "I think it's going to be a lot of fun, as long as I can get the sound out of my head of tiny little pilots calling *mayday mayday mayday*. But I'd like to know where they find such small test pilots."

"I think we should stick to model trains, Bud. They crash in fewer dimensions," Doc said. "By the way, nice suspenders. Who's *GW*? They make you look slimmer."

Bud replied, "That's because they're kind of like a girdle and help hold it all in."

"Let's watch the show, then go over to my place for a bit," Howie said. "I have a new song I want to play for you guys."

"That sounds great," Bud said, grinning, for it appeared the day was shaking out to be an improvement on the previous one, though he knew his luck could turn at any moment.

10

"Man, I feel guilty sitting around having fun while the women are all working," Howie said, leaning back in a plastic blue Adirondack-style chair on his front porch, his Maine coon cat Tobie in his lap. "We should do something nice for them when they get back from the cafe."

Doc replied, "What do you have in mind?"

"I don't know," Howie replied. "Maybe some flowers?"

"Where would we get flowers?" Doc asked. "I doubt if Sherwyn has any at the grocery store this early in the season. Maybe we could fix them dinner."

Petting Howie's other Maine coon cat, Bodie, Bud replied, "I doubt if they're going to be hungry after working in the cafe. But that's a great idea, Howie, if we can just think of something. In the meantime, what do you fellas think of this?"

Bud pulled an envelope from his pocket and handed it to Howie, saying, "This is the strange letter I mentioned that says the perfect crime is about to be committed."

Howie read the letter while Bud explained to Doc the events of the past few days, including finding Ted's body.

Looking troubled, Doc said, "Bud, every time I get around you I end up in the middle of some kind of mystery, like that weird cult up in Montana, and now here we go again."

Howie looked up, saying, "The sheriff's a mystery magnet, Doc. Everyone knows that. But Bud, this letter really is odd. I don't know what to make of it. Are you sure it's not some kind of prank?"

"I'm not sure of anything at this point, Howie. Let Doc read it, and let's see what he thinks."

After reading it, Doc said, "This is like something a high-schooler would write, Bud. It's kind of pushing it on the rhyming and cadence, not to mention the dramatic quality."

"Exactly," Howie replied. "I think Vinnie Pratt wrote it."

"He's in middle school, Howie," Bud replied.

"He's kind of precocious, Bud. It could've been him."

"What would be the point?" Bud asked.

Doc replied, "Whoever wrote it, I think the big clue's in the Van Gogh references. Do you know anyone who's into Van Gogh?"

"One of the couple who reported the death was wearing a Van Gogh t-shirt," Bud replied. "I found it interesting, but it's probably just a coincidence. But it could be any of these visiting artists."

"Can't ever assume anything in this biz," Doc replied. "Did this Ted guy have any enemies?"

"I don't know, but he was generally well-liked around town," Bud said. "I went by his house earlier. His lawn guy was there but didn't know where anyone was. I still need to notify his wife, but she was gone. But Doc, you're a doctor and used to be coroner. What would you suspect when someone died and had no apparent wounds or anything? Natural causes?"

"That would be my first guess, Bud," Doc replied. "But it could be anything from something natural like a heart attack to someone poisoning him."

"I guess we won't know until we hear back from the coroner. But why would his camera be all beat up? I know Ted took good care of his stuff."

Howie replied, "And Bud, don't forget, he had a drone case in his truck. Where's the drone?"

"Did you find the controller?" Doc asked.

"No, but we only looked around the cave. Maybe he dropped it somewhere."

"Or hid it," Howie added. "What if he was being threatened by someone?"

"I think he died of a heart attack or something," Bud said. "But what would this have to do with the letter? If someone were going to commit a perfect crime, they would make sure there was no body to be found, right?"

"Unless they were trying to frame someone else," Doc replied.

Bud added, "Then it wouldn't be a perfect crime. But this really strange fellow came and registered at the B&B the same day we found Ted's body."

"What was strange about him?" Doc asked.

"I don't know. I guess it was more the way he was dressed—he was pretty much covered from head to toe. Molly said he told her he had a skin problem and couldn't get any sun."

Howie said, "Maybe he was the Invisible Man, Sheriff. He had to cover himself from head to toe so nobody would notice he was invisible."

Bud was silent, then said, "Molly said the same thing, only that he was a ghost. I guess anything is possible at this point."

Doc replied, "I'm not making much sense of any of this, and it's making my head hurt. Let's go back to figuring out something nice for the gals."

"Some epsom salts for soaking their feet," Howie offered.

"Hows about some ice-cream shakes from Howie's?" Bud grinned. "We could also treat ourselves."

"I've got it!" Doc exclaimed. "How about we give them tomorrow off to go do whatever they want?"

"How would that work?" Bud asked. "Especially with all these tourists in town wanting to eat—needing to eat. We can't close the cafe down. Wilma Jean would never stand for it."

"We'll run the cafe ourselves," Doc replied.

"That sounds like a recipe for disaster," Bud said.

Howie grinned. "It sounds like a good way to get folks to come try Mayor Howie's Drive-In."

Bud said, "I can serve, or at least I think I can, and I know how to run a cash register, but if I cook, people could end up dying. Can you cook, Doc?"

"I actually enjoy cooking, Bud. I think I could handle it."

"What about Maureen?" Howie asked. "I can't do the drive-in alone, and she deserves a day off, too."

"I'll get Kale to come help you, Howie. I'm sure he can do basic stuff, though you'll probably have to teach him how to run a cash register."

"That's your hired hand on the farm?" Doc asked.

"He actually manages it now, Doc, since I'm so busy. I think he'll help us out when we tell him what's going on."

"What about Molly?" Howie asked.

"I'm not sure we could get anyone to cover for her with the B&B being so busy. She can take some time off when things settle down," Bud replied.

"Can you take a day off work?" Doc asked Bud.

"I just had my day off, but I can forward the office phone to my cell as a backup," Bud replied. "I think it's a great idea, as long as I can get Wilma Jean to agree. If she knows you're cooking and not me, Doc, she'll probably be OK with it. I know she's pretty burned out."

"It's a plan, then," Howie said, Tobie jumping off his lap as he stood. "You fellas mind if I get my guitar? I'd like to share a new song I wrote and see what you think."

He was soon back, guitar in hand, and started singing:

> I woke up one morning,
> All distraught and gray,
> And I looked up above,
> Saying, show me the way.
> Nothing but silence,
> So I asked my dog,
> And he said, OK,

I'll show you the way.
The way of the biscuit,
The way of the toy,
The way of the chewy,
The way of true joy.
The way of no worries,
I'll show you the way,
But you just have one day,
If you don't get it by then,
There's not much to say.
So we slept in the shade,
Licked ourselves and played ball,
Chased the cat and chewed chewies,
Dug a hole in the wall.
It was then that I got it,
Pure simplicity I say,
Don't worry, be happy,
And just live for the day.

Bud and Doc laughed while clapping.

"Howie that was great!" Bud said, trying to sound sincere.

"Great wisdom, my boy," Doc added.

"But hows come you're not writing about cats?" Bud asked. "I thought you were more of a cat aficionado."

Howie put his guitar down, saying, "I'm trying to warm Maureen up to the idea of getting a dog, Bud. I love my cats, but I've always wanted a dog." He paused, listening, then added, "But it sounds like the gals are here. Let's spring our idea on them and see what they say."

"Tomorrow, they can just live for the day," Doc said, grinning, as they opened the door and went out to meet them.

11

Bud leaned attentively against the cash register in the Melon Rind Cafe, checking to make sure no one needed anything. He knew a few of the patrons, but most were new faces, and he suspected they were either artists or radio-control pilots and fans.

A patron who Bud thought he recognized, but wasn't quite sure, said, "Hey, Bud, I thought you were our sheriff. Where's Wilma Jean?"

"She has the day off. I'm covering for her."

"Well," the man laughed, "If your apron there is true, I think all I want is a glass of iced tea."

"This is the only one I could find," Bud said with chagrin, looking down at his apron, which read, *I cook as good as I look.* He added, "Besides, I'm not actually the cook."

He now remembered the guy was the driver of the Schwann's truck, which delivered frozen food to people's houses, and added, "My only other choice was one that says *I like to party, and by party I mean take naps.* As sheriff, I prefer not to divulge my personal life. But why are you, of all people, eating here? Don't you buy your own product?"

"I need a break sometimes," the man replied. "And by sometimes, I mean about three times a day."

Bud now could see someone outside carrying a small camera with a microphone attached, apparently filming the Melon Rind Cafe sign and Wilma Jean's plastic petunias by the front door. The man then opened the door and came inside, still filming, followed by another man carrying a notebook.

The cameraman asked, "Is it OK to film you doing your serving job for a few minutes?"

Bud wasn't sure what to say—what if his constituents saw him moonlighting in the cafe? Finally, after some thought, he replied, "Probably not such a good idea."

"Why not?" The man persisted, all the while still filming. He added, "It's legal to record someone in a public place as long as they don't have a reasonable expectation of privacy. And generally in public, one doesn't have a reasonable expectation of privacy and so you can record people."

"Repeating it in a different way doesn't give it validity," Bud replied. "But you're actually not in a public place. This is a private business."

The man turned his camera off, saying, "It's definitely a public place. The public can come here and eat, right?"

Not wanting to get into an argument with the guy, Bud said softly, "Look fellas, this place is by invitation only. No filming."

Now looking hurt, the cameraman said, "But Mike here said we could take a break and have lunch."

Bud said, "OK, look. I'll give you an invite, but only if you don't film. Go ahead and take that booth over there."

They both looked relieved, putting their equipment on the table and studying the menu.

Just then, Bud noticed Kate and Charles coming in the door. He quickly ducked into the kitchen, where Doc was frying hamburgers.

"Doc, switch places with me for a bit, would you? That couple I mentioned earlier who found Ted Henderson's body just came in."

"Are you worried you're next?" Doc asked.

Bud handed Doc his apron and ticket book, saying, "I'll cook until they leave. Pretend to be cleaning tables or something. You can come check on things to make sure I'm doing it right. Hang around them and see if you can get any scuttlebutt. If they know I'm here they'll clam up."

"Scuttlebutt?"

"You know, Doc, gossip, rumor, that sort of thing."

"I know what it is, Bud. I was just wondering if you'd gone sailor on me."

"Sailor?"

"Scuttlebutt's an old nautical term for cask, like a water cooler, where the gossip flows. But you need to pay attention if we switch. Cooking's not for sissies, you know."

With that, Doc disappeared into the dining room while Bud studied the tickets to see what had been ordered.

In a few minutes, Doc popped back in, handing Bud another ticket, then quickly flipped the burgers on the grill.

"These were about to burn, Sheriff."

"I know, I was getting to them," Bud said defensively. "I can only do one thing at a time."

"And therein lies the reason you're not a cook," Doc replied. "But Bud, the woman seems very upset."

"Doc, get back out there and see why."

"They want lunches to go, Bud. Make some sandwiches and put chips and a soda with them. And those two fellows with the camera want patty melts and fries. I'll be right back."

Doc disappeared again as Bud put the burgers on two plates and began pouring gravy over them. He then opened a can of peaches and put a few on each plate as garnish, accidentally dropping them into the gravy, then began making the lunches.

Doc was soon back.

"They were talking about some painting, Bud. She said she recognizes the style, whatever that means. The guy then said, 'It's impossible, he's dead,' and she said she definitely knows that style. She seemed very upset. He started talking about their dogs, almost as if trying to divert her."

"Dogs? They have dogs? What kind?"

"They didn't say. Is that something important? They apparently left them home, because she then started worrying about them and whether or not someone—didn't get the name—was taking proper care of them."

"They have dogs," Bud replied. "Funny, I never took them as the type to have dogs."

"Bud, I think I should take over now. I'm going to have to redo those two plates. They just wanted patty melts, not peach-gravy burgers."

"Well, it should be on the menu, Doc," Bud said, putting the apron back on. "It actually sounds kind of good."

"I'll save them and you can try them later when things slow down," Doc replied.

Bud went back into the dining room with a carafe of coffee, filling people's cups and checking to see if anyone needed anything, avoiding the couple. The woman still seemed distraught, and her husband was trying to comfort her.

Bud listened in, pretending to clean the table behind them.

"Look, there's no way he painted that Datura. It's just impossible."

"I know that style, Charles, it has to be him."

"It doesn't make sense. His style isn't that unique—it had to be someone else. How could a dead man sneak in at night and paint something without being seen?"

"By sneaking in at night."

"They lock the doors. Nobody's going to sneak in, and ghosts can't paint. Look, I'll talk to Molly when we get back. Let's just go on out and have a nice day painting."

Doc came out of the kitchen with the two sack lunches, rang up their bill, and they were soon gone, still not noticing Bud.

"I didn't know you could operate a cash register," Bud said, relieved.

"Like you, I learned on the job, when Millie had the cafe. I'm a man of many talents." He nodded towards the door. "Isn't this guy coming in the one you mentioned when we were at Howie's?"

Bud watched as the man who he was now calling the Invisible

Man walked in the door. The man nodded at Bud and Doc, then took the empty table Bud had just cleaned as Doc went back into the kitchen.

Bud handed him a menu, asking, "Can I get you a drink?"

A muffled voice said, "I could use a drink—a real drink. A cup of coffee, please, black."

As the man spoke, Bud studied him carefully, noting that his forehead and cheeks weren't covered and seemed to be real skin—he then shook his head at himself for even considering what Howie had said about the guy being invisible.

Bringing the man a cup of coffee, Bud asked. "Ready to order?"

"I'd like a BLT. Hold the L and T. To go."

"You just want bread with bacon?"

"Yes, with a little mayo. Extra crispy, please."

"That comes with fries. Say, didn't I see you out at the B&B yesterday? Are you enjoying your stay?" Bud asked congenially.

"No, I mean yes. It's a nice enough place, but all those artists are irritating."

"You're not an artist?"

"I'm just here to see the countryside. Just a tourist."

Bud couldn't help but ask, "Have you been to Black Dragon Canyon yet? It's quite the place. Petroglyphs, if you're into that kind of thing."

The man looked up at Bud with a steady gaze, saying, "I have been there. It's quite memorable."

Bud nodded his head, then turned and handed the man's order to Doc. He was now distracted, thinking about how the Invisible Man wasn't wearing gloves and had a bandage on his hand.

Just then, his phone rang.

"Yell-ow."

"Is this the sheriff?" A woman's voice asked.

"It is. Can I help you?"

"Sheriff, my name's Rachael Henderson. I've been up in Salt Lake visiting my daughter, and when I came back home, my husband was nowhere to be found. His medicine is here, and he hasn't watered my flowers for what looks like several days. I'm worried sick about him."

"You're over on Cherry Street, right?"

"Yes."

"I'll be there as soon as I can find someone to cover for me," Bud replied.

He then dialed his friend Karen over at the Chow Down to see if her daughter Heather could come work for an hour or so.

It didn't take Heather long to show up, and Bud handed her his apron, saying he'd be back as soon as possible. He knew the cafe was in good hands, for Heather had worked off and on for Wilma Jean for some time and knew the routine.

He told Doc what was going on and slipped out the door. He would be glad to get a little time away from the cafe, having gained a new appreciation for what his wife did, but he sure wasn't very eager to go tell Rachael Henderson her husband was dead.

But maybe she could shed some light on why Ted would be staying at the B&B while she was gone visiting her sister, though Bud had an inkling that maybe it was something she might be better off not knowing.

He didn't want to upset her any further, especially since the news of her husband's death was bad enough, but he was beginning to think Ted staying at the B&B might have something to do with his death, and he needed to be thorough.

As he drove over to Cherry Street, he had the nagging feeling that something just wasn't quite right, that things were getting discombobulated to the point of pure chaos.

As he approached Ted's tidy foursquare house, one he knew had come from the old mining town of Sego, he flashed again on the photo of the canyon wall with the faint distortion with the blues and reds and yellows.

It was then that he recalled what Charles and Kate had been wearing when they'd come into his office: a blue shirt and a yellow and red-striped polo shirt.

Pulling up in front of Ted's house and ringing the doorbell, it was then that he knew he'd just made some kind of connection, if he could only make sense of it.

But at that moment, he knew he needed to do one of the things that he hated most about his job—telling someone their loved one was dead. It was second only to finding a body, and he wanted nothing more than to be out at the farm with the dogs, playing in the irrigation ditch, just living for the day.

12

___

Bud could see a nice sunset was in the making, which he'd suspected might happen from the high wispy clouds he'd noticed upon leaving Ted Henderson's house.

He'd picked up Doc at the cafe and they'd come to the equipment shed on the farm to see if they could find Kale. He was curious as to how his hired hand's day had gone at Howie's Drive-In. But since Kale wasn't there, they'd decided to just hang out and enjoy the peace and quiet.

Wilma Jean and Millie had showed up at the cafe just as Bud returned from talking to Rachael Henderson, saying they'd come back early to see if the cafe was still standing.

They'd caught Bud in the kitchen talking to Doc and eating a bowl of vanilla-bean ice cream while Heather, the high-school girl he'd called to come waitress, was busy taking orders.

Wilma Jean had commented about Bud delegating his work to others, then had promptly run both him and Doc out of the kitchen. Bud hadn't minded one bit, though he'd acted like he was hurt.

Now he kind of wished he'd stopped by the bungalow and picked up the dogs, but on the other hand, it was kind of nice not having to pay attention to anything for once, to just let his mind wander. The day had been hectic, and having to go tell Rachael Henderson her husband was dead hadn't been all that much fun, either. He was tired and just wanted to sit—or maybe vegetate was a better word for it, he mused.

Rachael had been a pleasant-enough woman, well-dressed with hints of gray in her hair, and she'd seemed to take the message as well as could be expected. Bud had told her he was keeping Ted's camera gear until he was sure it had no evidence, and he also told her where Howie had hid the keys to Ted's truck when he'd returned it.

But even though he hadn't wanted to, he'd had to ask why Ted would be staying at the Melon View B&B, and this hadn't set well with Rachael, who'd said she had no idea why. She said that her husband often spent the night out in remote areas to get night-sky photos, but he'd never mentioned staying at the B&B, and was he sure it had really been Ted?

He'd also asked her to look around the house to be sure Ted hadn't left his drone there, mentioning they'd found the empty case in Ted's pickup. She'd said she would call if she found it, and at that point, Bud had left, feeling bad about leaving her alone, though she was going to call her daughter in Salt Lake and see if she could come down.

Bud sat down in the old office chair he used for working on equipment, wheeled it over to the work desk, and picked up what he knew had to be a drone controller, even though he'd never seen one before.

Millie had handed it to Doc as they'd left the cafe, saying she'd found it in Black Dragon Canyon. The women had gone for a hike there, since everyone was talking about it so much.

Now Doc, who'd also been watching the sunset, said, "Bud, my nephew Rich has a drone. He let me try it out a few times, so I know just enough about them to be dangerous."

"Is there any way we could take this controller back out in the canyon and somehow use it to call the drone back from wherever it is?" Bud asked. "Assuming it's still out there."

"It's probably still there, seeing how the controller was," Doc replied. "But the thing with drones is, they always come back to the controller when you turn it off. That's so if your batteries die you don't lose it. So the drone should've been right where they found the controller."

Bud replied, "I asked the gals, and they said they looked around and didn't find it. Do you think someone picked it up?" He was now running his thumbs up and down his suspenders, fiddling with them.

Doc replied, "It could've gone rogue, but that's rare. Drones anymore are very reliable, and this looks like one of the newer ones. The only other thing is, maybe Ted moved after the controller died or was turned off. The drone would go back to the same GPS coordinates that it recorded when it was launched. That's how they work."

"So the drone could be anywhere, huh Doc?"

"Well, yes, anywhere within its range. Most of them have ranges of several miles, though the newer ones can go much farther."

"We'll probably never find it then," Bud said.

"Well, there is one way we might figure out where he launched it and then go see if it returned itself there. The controller has an SD card that records what the camera in the drone sees. We should be able to download the video it took and maybe see where it last was. But Bud, are you thinking the drone's going to have something important to show us? Usually drone pilots just fly them around for the scenery. And if Ted was murdered, it seems like they would take the drone just in case he'd filmed them."

Bud answered, "That seems likely, especially if they didn't know the controller also recorded the images as a backup. Or maybe they couldn't find the controller. Either way, I don't know if the drone would have some useful information, Doc, but I need to find it to be sure. I want to go on back to the bungalow and see if I can download the pictures from the controller's SD card. You guys are staying with us, right?"

Doc replied, "No, Millie said Wilma Jean called Molly and a room opened up at the B&B. I told Millie I'd have you drop me off there, and she's going to drive on out when she's done at the cafe."

"That sounds fine," Bud replied. "Keep an eye on things out there, will you? I have no thoughts yet about what happened out in Black Dragon, maybe nothing at all, but since you'll be out there where everyone's staying, let me know if you hear anything."

Bud knew Doc was tired and ready to call it a day, so he grabbed the controller, and they were soon on their way to the B&B, the sunset now making everything glow a rich orange. Once there, Bud went inside with Doc to be sure the room was ready.

Molly was watering the plants in the big living room, and upon seeing Bud and Doc, said, "You guys are in luck, Doc. You're getting the nicest room in the house. It was the original master bedroom and the only one downstairs. Let me show you, then I need to get busy making some cinnamon rolls for breakfast, which is at eight sharp, by the way."

Bud said goodbye as Doc and Molly went into the back room, then paused for a moment to look at the painting by the fireplace. Someone had added a beautiful pastel blue to the sky, which made the wispy clouds stand out.

Thinking of what the couple had said in the cafe about unique style, he also noted a canyon wall had been added in the background, and someone had painted a beautiful creamy-white Datura flower in the foreground, complete with a hawkmoth hovering over it. Looking closer, he could see that it was indeed in a style somewhat different from the rest, much more impressionistic.

A voice behind Bud said, "Did you know that the word easel comes from the Dutch word *ezel*, meaning donkey? The Dutch called the easel a donkey because, like a beast of burden, it lugged the artist's canvas from one spot to another."

Bud turned to see Charles.

"I didn't know that," he replied. "The Dutch were pretty important in art history, weren't they?"

"Oh yes, indeed," Charles replied. "The Dutch Golden Age of painting from about 1620 to 1680 saw a very distinct style developed, though it was deeply influenced by Flemish Baroque painting. The seventeenth century saw some of the most important advances in art, all in Dutch cities."

"Was that when Van Gogh lived?" Bud asked, studying Charles' reaction.

"No, no, he lived much later, in the late 1800s, though he was one of the most famous and influential figures in art history. He created about 2,100 artworks, all characterized by bold colors and dramatic brushstrokes."

"But he was Dutch, right?" Bud asked. "I really don't know much about art."

"You don't need to know anything to enjoy it. We are the artists of our own lives."

Bud continued, "If that's true, mine doesn't have much going for it except some local color. But looking at this painting you guys are working on, that Datura and hawkmoth are different from the rest, maybe kind of impressionistic, like Van Gogh's style? Didn't he die under mysterious circumstances?"

"I believe he killed himself," Charles answered, now seeming unsettled and turning to go. "I need to go find my wife. Nice talking with you."

Bud knew he needed to talk to Charles and Kate more about finding Ted out in the canyon, but he wanted to hear back from the coroner first. He said goodnight to Doc and Molly, then drove down the long farm lane, the sunset now having turned into a distant glow on the horizon as the shadows lengthened.

Almost back to the main road, he came upon someone riding a bicycle, his headlights showing a young guy with light blonde hair. He almost stopped to warn him about riding in the dark with no reflector or lights, then continued on, tired and wanting to get home to check on the dogs, thinking about Charles' reaction to him asking about Van Gogh's death.

13

It was the next morning, and Bud leaned against the counter of the Melon Rind Cafe as he patiently waited for his wife to finish talking to a customer.

Doc and Howie waited outside in Doc's black Land Rover. The trio had decided to go out to Black Dragon Canyon and search for the drone, though they wanted to get back in time to go to the RC show at the airport.

Bud listened in on the conversation between Wilma Jean and an older gentleman who was dressed in a dark brown leather jacket, a red neck scarf, and wore what looked to be a black leather German aviator cap with a plastic visor.

The man, speaking in what Bud took to be a German accent, said, "I think it's fantastic that you're a pilot, too. We need more women pilots. What do you fly?"

"A Cessna Skyhawk," Wilma Jean replied.

"Did you build it yourself?"

Wilma Jean laughed incredulously. "I'm not that mechanically talented, yet alone have that kind of time."

"What color is it?" The man asked.

"It's bright pink," she smiled.

Surprised, the man replied, "Pink? That's certainly unusual. Did you at least paint it yourself?"

"Gosh no, That would be quite the job. I had our airport guy do it. He's very good at stuff like that."

"Well, OK then, I guess one doesn't have to be handy to be in the sport, though most of us build and paint our own. Do you crash very often?"

"Crash? Heavens no! I've never crashed."

The man leaned back in his booth, saying, "Well, you will. It's just part of the learning curve. Sometimes Gravity enters the chat uninvited, and more often than not Murphy is with him. I've seen lots of devastating crashes, and my heart goes out to the victims. I grew up with it, and sometimes my dad would crash, and then he'd cry. Sometimes it would be a perfect landing, but with the landing gear left back on the runway somewhere. The whole family would be depressed for days."

Wilma Jean said, "Oh my gosh! That sounds terrible! But what do you fly?"

"I have a blimp. It's modeled after the Hindenburg."

"You fly a blimp? I've never met a blimp pilot. I've heard they're quite expensive."

"Not really. I built it myself."

"You built a blimp? Unbelievable! I've heard it costs over $100,000 just to fill them with helium."

"Oh, ridiculous! Not even close. They're actually quite affordable."

"Where do you keep it?"

"Right now it's tethered out at the airport. The guy there let me put it in the hanger."

"Seriously? It actually fits? I'm going to have to go see it for myself. How long will it be there?"

"A few days."

Wilma Jean paused as if thinking, then added, "I hate to say it, but I hope it doesn't explode like the real one did."

"Oh, not a chance. See, they'd put hydrogen in the Hindenburg because they couldn't get helium. Hydrogen is quite explosive."

"Do you take up passengers?"

"Passengers? I guess if you had some photogenic models, I could do that, but generally, no."

Wilma Jean stood abruptly, saying, "Well, nice talking to you. I need to get back to work."

As the man walked out, she seemed irritated, whispering to Bud, "I was interested until he said he only took photogenic models up. He seemed kind of full of himself at that point."

Bud laughed. "Hon, you guys were having parallel conversations."

"How so?"

"He's a radio-control pilot. That's what he meant about building his own and painting it and crashing, as well as taking up models, like little Lego people wearing tiny parachutes or something. There's an RC show out at the airport. But I need to pick up our lunches. The guys are waiting in the car."

"Well, I'll be darned! A radio-controlled blimp! Will wonders never cease? Are you taking the dogs?"

"Just Lindie, as she stays with us instead of hunting all over like Pierre and Hoppie. We're going to have a picnic and see if we can find that drone."

As she handed Bud the lunches, she said, "By the way, Molly's looking for you. She said there was another to-do out at the B&B but it wasn't the usual characters, whatever that means, and to call her when you get a chance. She said it's over now, but she wants to ask you about it."

Bud groaned. He'd call her on the way out to Black Dragon, as they needed to get going if they wanted to make it back for the RC show, and besides, he didn't want to get diverted out to the B&B.

He and Doc and Howie were in Doc's Rover with Doc driving, well out of town, when Bud dialed Molly's number.

"Melon View B&B," Molly answered.

"Hello, Molly, Bud here. What's going on?"

"Oh Bud, I just had the strangest thing happen. I need your advice. I had just served breakfast and everyone was sitting down eating when this woman came in and asked for me, then started interrogating me in front of everyone. I had no idea what she was talking about, but she acted like I knew but wouldn't admit it. Right there in front of everyone."

Bud replied, "Who was it, Molly? And what did she say?"

"Oh, it was bad. Everyone heard it. She asked me if I knew her husband and then wanted to know why he would be coming out here to stay when he had a perfectly good home and wife in town, and I must know he was having an affair or something, and who was this other woman? Bud, I don't even know who her husband is. And she made it sound like I knew who his girlfriend was, or it was maybe even me."

"Wow, Molly! But I'm going to lose you soon," Bud replied, knowing they would soon be out of cell range. "Surely there's some reason behind this, some context. Is that all you know?"

"She then said her husband had just been found dead, and she knew this woman must've had something to do with it. Bud, this has to be the same guy that Kate and Charles found, and when they heard her, Kate jumped up and said 'Oh my God, he's remarried,' and ran upstairs crying, Charles following her. I haven't seen them since."

"Molly, was this woman's name Rachael?"

"I don't know, Bud. She stomped out crying and drove off. I swear, if things don't settle down, I'm going to take some time off and go stay with my sister in Bountiful, though I'd sure hate to leave Wilma Jean in a pickle."

"Now Molly, no need for that. If things get bad, I'll come stay out there."

"We don't have any rooms."

"Well, Doc's staying there. Next time, contact him. But like I said, I'm going to lose you."

"And Bud, that's not all. I discovered someone had cut a bunch of flowers from the planter out back. Some really beautiful red Indian paintbrush and pink Palmer's penstemon. I've been babying them forever and they were finally starting to do well. Bud, I discovered them in Charles and Kate's room this morning in a vase, and sure enough, it was *my* vase, too. They had to rummage around in the cupboard to even know it was there."

"But why would they do something like that?" Bud asked. "Surely they'd realize you would notice."

"They've been nothing but trouble. I wish they would leave."

"How much longer will they be here?" Bud asked.

But just then, the signal dropped, for they were nearing Black Dragon Canyon.

"That was an interesting conversation," Doc said, turning off the freeway. "Your side of it, anyway."

"Too interesting," Bud replied.

"And what's she supposed to contact me for next time? Did the plumbing back up or something? Have her call Howie," Doc grinned.

"I'm busy being mayor," Howie replied. "Have her call the sheriff."

Bud replied, "If this petty thievery keeps up, I *will* have to get involved."

He then got out to open the gate, only to find it had been padlocked shut.

14

Bud stood, running his thumbs up and down his suspenders, not sure what to do.

Who had padlocked the gate into Black Dragon, and why? It was public land, so no one had the right to lock it except the Bureau of Land Management, or BLM, who managed the area, and they couldn't lock it unless there was some kind of hazard or revegetation or something, and even then, they would post a sign.

Bud examined the lock—it was just a small padlock like one would use to lock a bicycle or tool chest or such, not a serious lock like a government agency would use.

Bud recalled being fascinated as a kid by Richard Feynman, who had helped tame atomic energy. Bud had been impressed not by Feynman's Nobel Prize winning brilliance in physics, but rather his ability to pick locks. Bud had gone through a period when he'd tried to emulate Feynman, developing various lock-picking techniques, but he'd eventually lost interest.

But his techniques had served him well not too long ago in another case, and he now wondered if he could again call upon what he'd learned to help him gain access into the canyon. He knew he would be well within his rights as a sheriff investigating a crime to just cut the lock, but his bolt cutters were in the sheriff's car, and he doubted if Doc carried a pair.

Trying to recall what he'd learned about combination locks, he absent-mindedly snapped his suspenders, which stung a bit, yet seemed to jar his memory. Hadn't he had good luck a few times using a small hammer?

He picked up a nearby rock and used it to tap the side of the lock, and presto, it fell open. He took the lock off, amazed at how easy it had been. He stuck it in his pocket, as he didn't want to come back and find someone had again locked them in, as it might not open as easily next time.

"What was that all about?" Doc asked as Bud got back into the vehicle.

"Someone doesn't want anyone in the canyon," Bud replied. "We might want to proceed with caution."

They drove on in silence until they finally reached the parking area near the petroglyphs. The canyon was empty with no other visitors, which was no surprise. Doc parked and they got out, Lindie sniffing around as Bud grabbed a water bottle.

"Did you have any luck downloading what was on the controller?" Doc asked. "Did it give any indication where to start looking?"

"I don't have an SD card reader," Bud replied. "I have the card, but no way to read it. But the drone can't be all that far, Doc. It only has a range of 2 miles, and the canyon's only a few hundred feet wide. I think it's unlikely that he would be flying it out of the canyon. It's probably not far from the cave."

Doc stood looking at the petroglyphs for a moment, then said, "It's been a long time since I was here, but I still don't see how they got a dragon out of that. But have you boys ever heard of the Black Dragon Cafe?"

Howie and Bud said they hadn't, and Doc continued.

"Well, back when they were blasting the freeway through Spotted

Wolf Canyon, they decided to use the Black Dragon area as a camp site, since it was basically at the base of the Swell near where they were working. Most of the camp was just canvas tents, but they hired an old sheepman as a cook. Now, this fellow had run sheep in here years before, so he decided to resurrect an old cabin he'd built back then, even though it was about to fall down. He moved into it while he was working as a cook, and once the project was completed, he stayed. He tried to make a living serving food to mostly nobody, and he finally gave up and left. But he called it the Black Dragon Cafe. There used to be a sign by the freeway. Lots of people got stuck trying to get to it, so the highway department finally took the sign down. The old cabin was just up the canyon here a few hundred feet. I wonder if there's still anything left of it."

"How do you know all this, Doc?" Howie asked.

"Well, before I quit as coroner and married Millie and moved to Colorado, I would go over to Salina once a week to volunteer at their low-income clinic. I got a call from them one day asking me to stop in here because someone had reported the old guy was sick as a dog and needed help."

"Was I sheriff then?" Bud asked.

"No, this was probably a good five years before your time. So I stopped in here, had no idea really where I was going as I had never been here before, and found the old guy on his deathbed. I managed to get him to the hospital in Salina, where he eventually recovered. He had a bad case of salmonella. I don't know where he went after that."

"Sounds like he shouldn't have been eating his own cooking," Howie commented. "I wonder how many highway workers he killed."

"Lack of refrigeration will do that to one," Bud said. "But let's get going. We can walk in a kind of grid. I'll take this side of the canyon, Howie can do the middle, and Doc, you do the other side."

They set off, eyes glued to the ground, searching through piles of rock rubble, stands of rabbitbrush, and grasses, though it was mostly just sand where the wash wound through the canyon. Lindie was having a blast wandering, though she stayed close.

Bud was wishing he'd brought his camera, as the claret-cup cactus was in bloom, and its rich red blossoms stood out clear across the canyon. He was caught up in studying one when Lindie growled.

Lindie never growled at much of anything, except when Pierre was trying to steal her biscuit. Bud looked up to see a small wiry man wearing dirty green coveralls and a baseball cap standing on the cliff some 30 feet above him, looking down. His long hair stuck out from under the cap, backlit by the sun.

"Lose somethin'?" He asked in a voice that somehow matched the threadbare look of his faded green coveralls, kind of scratchy and beat-up and worn sounding. Bud noted he had a long red mark on his hand, as if he'd been cut by a knife or something sharp.

"Yes, we did," Bud replied, startled. "Have you seen a drone around?"

The man quickly slid down the steep slope on his rear, Bud wondering how he kept from tearing holes in his pants. Bud could now see he was gray-haired and thin and wondered if he wasn't looking at the same sheepherder Doc had mentioned.

"It's over in the bushes," the man said, pointing to a stand of rabbitbrush across the canyon. "I was waiting to hear if I should destroy it or not. How did you get in here?"

"Are you the one who locked the gate?" Bud asked, suspecting he already knew the answer.

"Did you break my lock?" the man asked.

Pulling the lock from his pocket, Bud handed it to the man, asking, "What authority do you have to lock up public lands?"

"How'd you get it open without breaking it?" The man asked, perplexed. "Yes, I was told to lock the place up. It's getting too busy. The wrong crowd's coming in. But how did you get this open?"

By now, both Howie and Doc had come over to where Bud and the man stood.

"This fellow—say, I didn't get your name—says the drone's over in the rabbitbrush," Bud said.

"My name's Scratch. But say, have you ever thought about how the only reason most people know their own names is because other people told them who they are? Everybody could be somebody completely different from who they think they are. And who are you fellas?"

"Well, I'm Bud, this is Doc, and this is Howie," Bud replied. "But who told you to lock up the canyon?"

"The Great Attractor," Scratch replied.

"I've heard John Deere makes a great tractor," Doc replied.

Ignoring him, Scratch continued. "I've been living out here off and on for ages, keeping an eye on the place for the Great Attractor, and now he's getting upset—or maybe he's a she, or even an it. I don't wanna be disrespectful, so I'll call him or her an it, and capitalize it to show honor to It. We must honor the Great Attractor, for we all will someday be in Its bosom, all One, all together merged into Its Great Attraction."

"Is that It's with an apostrophe, or Its without?" Doc asked.

Scratch looked confused, then said, "I think I know you from somewhere. You been in here before?"

Not wanting to get sidetracked, Bud asked, "Would you mind showing us where the drone is?"

"I need to ask if it's OK, first," Scratch replied, now scratching Lindie's neck under her collar, the dog looking like she'd died and gone to Heaven, her leg scratching in unison.

"You know, the best things in life aren't free, they're furry," Scratch said. "I wish I had a dog."

Trying to get him back on track, Bud asked, "Who do you need to ask if we can have the drone?"

Scratch gave him a sidelong look. "Like I said, the Great Attractor. You fellas go on over there a ways so I can commune properly."

"OK," Bud replied. "Tell you what, we brought our lunches with us, so we'll go have lunch while you're communing."

"Lunch? Well, I actually commune even better over food. Maybe I can join you. We can go eat at the Black Dragon Cafe."

Now pretty sure he was talking to the old sheepherder, Bud nodded in agreement, saying, "We have plenty. We'll follow you."

With that, Scratch led them down the canyon, past the cave, across the wash, and under a small grove of ancient cottonwood trees where an old dilapidated cabin was slowly melting into the canyon duff.

15

Bud sat on an old log and opened his sack lunch, which held two roast-beef sandwiches, some chips, a can of root beer, a pickle, and a small cup of potato salad.

Handing Scratch one of the sandwiches, he asked, "When was the last time you had something to eat? You look kind of hungry."

"I don't remember the last time I had real food like this," Scratch replied, chomping into the sandwich with great relish.

"What do you eat out here?" Doc asked. "Bugs?"

Scratch frowned, saying, "You must think I'm a real barbarian. I only eat bugs when there's nothing else, like lizards." He then laughed, adding, "Just kidding. I'm a vegetarian. Lots of plants to eat on, like cactus fruit. Sometimes tourist types will share with me, and I have a couple of friends that bring me stuff from town."

"Vegetarian? But you're eating roast beef," Howie said. "Where do you get water?"

"There's a nice seep over in Double Arch Canyon," Scratch replied, ignoring the comment about roast beef.

Before Bud could even take a bite from his sandwich, Scratch had downed his and was eyeing Bud's. Bud handed it all to him, saying,

"You can have the rest. I'm not hungry, and I can eat when we get back into town."

"It'll make those suspenders fit better if you cut back on stuff like this," Scratch informed him, smiling a toothy smile while taking the sack, starting on the second sandwich. "Is *GW* your initials?"

Howie now also handed his sack lunch to Scratch, saying, "Here, you need this more than I do. I can eat back in town later."

Doc handed him his lunch, too, and Scratch, looking surprised, said, "Well, fellas, I sure appreciate this."

"We need to find that drone," Bud said. "Are you done communing?"

Scratch grinned. "The best way to commune is to lie on the ground in the dark, watching the sky while talking softly after having a nice cup of tea. I never build campfires, for watching a campfire reduces one's field of perception, makes our world tiny. Watching the sky expands our perceptions and makes our world infinite."

"I think I would enjoy that," Bud replied. "But what about this Great Attractor fella—excuse me—It. Is it going to let you give us the drone?"

"That's an It with a capital I, don't forget," Scratch said, his mouth now full of potato salad.

Howie looked thoughtful, then asked, "Is this the anomaly that's the central gravitational point of the Laniakea Supercluster?"

Doc explained, "Howie's an amateur astronomer. He actually discovered a comet not too long ago."

Scratch looked surprised. "It sounds like you're part of the Brotherhood, or maybe I should say the It-Hood. I don't meet many others in the It-Hood, in fact, you're the first, except my friend who up and left."

"I know a little about it," Howie replied. "But I'm not part of the It-Hood or whatever you call it. I just know that astronomers can observe anomalies that suggest a concentration of mass millions of times more massive than the Milky Way, and they call it the Great Attractor. It's obscured by our own Milky Way's galactic plane, so we can't see it. This plane is called the Zone of Avoidance."

"Is that like the Zone of Death?" Doc asked. "You know, that place in Yellowstone where you can commit a crime and not be prosecuted?"

Scratch, ignoring him, said to Howie, "Yes, you are definitely part of the It-Hood to understand so much. It attracts us all, and someday we will all be in Its bosom forever. Until then we have to just believe in the great mystery."

Howie replied, "But it's not really a mystery. It's simply gravitational attraction by a large mass."

Scratch stood, holding onto the sack lunches for dear life as Lindie begged for a bite, and said, "There are many ways to explain It. The main thing is that you believe and are faithful to It. And you capitalize It. I like being out here away from the action because I can feel the Great Attractor deeper. There's nothing to distract me. And out here people don't ask too many questions. So what are you doing out here, anyway?"

Doc replied, "I thought out here people didn't ask too many questions."

Scratch said, "Yes, the operative words are too many, not none. It's OK to have a few questions."

Howie added, "In another hundred million years Earth will be on the other side of the Milky Way Galaxy, allowing us to see past the galactic plane."

Bud said, "I don't think we'll be around at that point, Howie." He turned to Scratch and added, "But we're out here looking for that drone. Can we go retrieve it now? We need to get back to town."

"It's over in those bushes, like I said," Scratch replied with irritation. "Go get it." He then put a small bite of his sandwich back into the sack. Seeing Bud's questioning look, he added, "See, if I save a bite, I can fool myself into thinking I still have some left. But I guess I actually *do* have some left this time, with these other sandwiches."

As Howie and Doc went to look in the rabbitbrush, Bud asked Scratch, "Hows come you know where it is? Did you see it go down?"

"I did," Scratch said, unconcerned.

"Didn't it belong to Ted Henderson?" Bud asked.

"I dunno," Scratch said. "Somebody was in here flying it around, and I saw it whirring around on the ground like it was going crazy. I tried to catch it and it crashed, cut my hand. The Great Attractor told me to get rid of it—it was making too much noise."

"Scratch, was this guy kind of a big fellow, carrying a camera and taking photos?"

"Yes."

"Did you see anyone else in the canyon?"

"Yes, I did, and that's when the Great Attractor told me to lock it all up. Too many people, and they were pushing each other around and yelling and making too much noise."

"They were pushing each other around?"

"Yes, but over in Double Arch Canyon. There was a couple over there, a man and woman, and they were the ones pushing."

"Who did they push?"

"They pushed each other for awhile, then another guy was there and fell off the edge of a rock. It kind of looked like the woman pushed him, but I couldn't tell for sure. Then they took off, just leaving him there. I climbed down and went to check on him, but he was gone, so I don't know what happened. But these canyons are supposed to be a place of peace. The world's got too many crazy people, and we don't need them in here. So I locked it up."

Bud was quiet for a moment. He could see Doc and Howie coming back, carrying the drone. He then said, "The guy we call Doc, he saved your life once, if you're who I think you are. Do you remember when you ran the Black Dragon Cafe and a doctor came in and rescued you?"

Scratch looked surprised, then said, "That was a long time ago, but I knew I recognized him. I've never had a chance to thank him. I didn't even know who he was."

"Scratch, if I brought you a photo, could you identify the couple you saw in Double Arch?"

"Nah, they were too far away. Would you mind bringing me some more of those sack lunches?"

"Not a problem. And what did the guy look like that they pushed? Was it the photographer guy?"

"No, not him. I didn't get a good look, as like I said, they were too far off. But why are you so interested?"

Bud replied, "I just like to know what's going on."

"And I thought *I* was crazy. Why do you want to know what's going on way out here?"

"I'm the sheriff," Bud replied.

Scratch, looking troubled, said, "I didn't do anything wrong. I know I shouldn't have messed with the drone. The guy just left it, and I'm a curious kind of fella."

"It's OK, Scratch. We just need to see what's on it and then take it back."

"What do you mean what's on it?"

"It has a camera."

"You mean he was recording stuff out here?"

"Yes."

Scratch sat down on the old log and said, "Sheriff, I'm really not crazy. It's a hard life out here. I was doing OK until my girlfriend kicked me out. Now I have nowhere to go, and as you can see, I'm not getting any younger. I just don't know what's going to happen to me. And if there's anything on that camera, you need to just keep that in mind."

"What could be on the camera?" Bud asked.

"I don't know," Scratch replied. "Sometimes I look through people's stuff to see if they have food. I'm starving out here."

"Why don't you come into town? There are services there to help people like you. Things like Meals on Wheels—they bring you lunch every day. Maybe they can help you find a place to live, get on some kind of stipend or something."

"There's a place that brings you lunch? Is it free?"

"Yes."

"Would they bring me lunch out here?"

"I kind of doubt it," Bud replied.

Doc and Howie were now back, and Scratch said, "I understand you're the fella who saved my life. I can't thank you enough."

Doc looked surprised, then replied, "Anyone would've done it, my friend."

Scratch said hopefully, "You know, the Chinese say that once you've saved a person's life, you're responsible for them forever."

Doc laughed. "The Chinese say all kinds of crazy things. It's best to heed the sayings of the Irish. For example, you've got to do your own growing, no matter how tall your grandfather was. And here's another—you'll never plough a field by turning it over in your mind."

"I don't get it," Scratch replied.

"Something to think about out here all alone," Doc said.

"We have to get going," Bud added, handing Scratch a card with his number on it. "I know you don't have a phone, and there's no service in here anyway, but if you're ever in town, let me know and I'll see what we can do to help you out. But just don't go locking that gate again, Scratch."

"I won't," Scratch replied. "And I'm really not crazy, in spite of what you all must think."

They said goodbye, and as they headed back to Doc's Rover and on out the canyon, Bud wondered about the couple Scratch had mentioned, thinking he had a pretty good idea who they might be.

As he got out and opened the gate for Doc, Bud turned, looking back at the distant walls of Black Dragon Canyon, feeling a sense of sadness for Scratch, destitute and hungry out in the canyons, and like he said, not getting any younger.

16

Bud sat on the back porch of the bungalow, throwing the dogs a stick and drinking a cold glass of lemonade. He'd decided to go home instead of returning to the RC show with Doc and Howie, as he was tired and needed some time alone to think.

He'd taken off the suspenders, for they made him feel vaguely persecuted, like he wasn't disciplined enough to stay slim and trim, and he kept thinking of how his Uncle Junior needed suspenders to keep his pants up. Bud knew he wasn't quite at that stage yet, and he hoped to prevent it from ever happening. Since Junior was a good 30 years older, he figured he still had some time to change his ways— plenty of time.

The only problem now was that he didn't have anything to fiddle with. Fiddling with suspenders was a somewhat dangerous enterprise, and he wished he could remember where he'd left his harmonica.

Since all the glasses were in the dishwasher, he'd taken Wilma Jean's antique peacock crystal glass from her display case above the buffet. The glass was a beautiful work of art, especially when the sun shone through the peacock's tail painted on the crystal, and the yellow lemonade made the colors look even more ethereal.

He knew he'd be in big trouble if his wife caught him using it, which was a fact born of experience, having once almost destroyed it by leaving it on the town's watermelon float. But he also knew that Wilma Jean was busy at the cafe and wouldn't be home until late.

Bud leaned back, thinking of all that had happened in the past few days. It was somewhat unsettling, in that a lot of it didn't make sense, and he was used to solving mysteries that were more of the whodunnit variety than this, which was more of a whodunwhat.

He decided he should make a list of everything going on and see if he could make some sense of it. He started to get up to go get a tablet and pen, but Hoppie was now sleeping on his feet, and he didn't want to wake him, so he decided to see if he could do it all mentally, like one of those things that they say you should do to stave off dementia, like crossword puzzles and Sudoku, whatever that was.

Leaning back, he first thought of the strange letter he'd received about the perfect crime with its wax seal, which led him to wonder about the ring he'd found, which appeared to have been used to stamp that same seal.

Why was it in the cave where they'd found Ted's body? Was it just a coincidence, or was Ted somehow involved with the letter? If so, why would a fellow Green Riverite want to send a letter like that to the local sheriff?

And why was Ted staying at the Melon View B&B? Was he involved with someone there, or was he hiding out? And why was Kate so upset when she found out he was remarried when she herself was remarried? Was she still seeing her ex-husband? If so, why would she be upset after his wife Rachael came to the B&B and accused someone of having an affair with him? Was that someone Kate?

Bud desperately needed something to fiddle with, and since the lemonade was now gone, he began running his finger around the rim of the glass.

He now remembered that Charles' business card had said he was an insurance adjustor. Given what Scratch said about them pushing Ted off the rock, were they trying to kill him to get some kind of insurance? And what was on the drone's camera? He needed to examine it and see, but he was too tired right then. And what about the strange photo of the canyon wall with the dim colors?

As Bud thought, he fiddled more and more with the glass, running his finger around the rim until it began making a humming sound. Hoppie was now awake, ears cocked, and Lindie sat at Bud's feet, watching to see what he was doing. Pierre had run back into the house and hid.

And what about the strange guy called Hawk? He claimed to be a social entrepreneur, whatever that was. And there was no way he could actually be from Sego—nobody was from Sego, as the old coal-mining town had died many years before and all that was left were a few crumbling buildings.

Bud had visited it a number of times and knew exactly where the old town sat in Sego Canyon in the Bookcliffs, just a few miles from Thompson Springs. As far as he knew, it hadn't been inhabited since the 1950s.

The glass hummed louder and louder as Bud got the hang of it, though he was far removed in thought, not really noticing. Lindie was now trying to hide under his chair, and Hoppie had started whining.

Bud was now thinking about the Van Gogh t-shirt Charles was wearing, as well as his reaction when Bud had asked if the artist had been murdered, almost as if he thought Bud suspected him of something. And what about the Datura and hawkmoth on the canvas at the B&B? Who had painted it, and why had Kate been so upset by it?

Bud's thoughts now turned to the missing steaks and the vase Molly had discovered with her missing flowers. Was Joey the Green River Gopher responsible? Was he running errands for people, then pocketing the money and stealing whatever they'd ordered, like the steaks? Just one more thing he needed to look into.

But what bothered Bud the most was the letter that had seemed to originally set all this off. He needed to know if someone was intending to commit a perfect crime or not—or was Ted's murder that crime? If so, it wasn't even close to perfect, as there was a body, even if there wasn't a suspect—yet.

As if waking from a dream, Bud now realized the dogs were

howling and someone was asking what was going on and it was Wilma Jean and he'd been busted with the peacock glass—yet again —and she had someone with her who was laughing, actually more than one person laughing, in fact, it seemed like an entire crowd had appeared from nowhere.

Turning, Bud could see it was Doc and Millie, Howie and Maureen, Eldon, Frosty, and Eileen Jensen.

"Beautiful," Doc said. "I had no idea you were into glassical music."

"And the dogs make quite the chorus," Maureen added. "Can you play some Tchaikovsky? Something like the Dance of the Sugar Plum Fairies? Or did you lose your glasses?"

Everyone laughed but Wilma Jean, who said, "Hon, this is beyond the pale. That glass is a family heirloom."

Bud sighed, then said, "Hoppie made me do it. He wanted to do a sing-along. I lost my harmonica and I'm a desperate man at this point. But you do recall I was with you when you bought this at Wiggins Diggins, don't you?"

"Well," she replied. "It's *somebody's* family heirloom. And your harmonica is right where you left it in the freezer. I assumed it was there for a reason so I left it. But come on inside. I brought dinner from the cafe—your favorite—enchiladas. Then we're having the wedding rehearsal in the yard."

"And you missed out on a very entertaining afternoon at the airport," Doc added. "The blimp crashed, and they had a guy with a radio-controlled ambulance come in. It was really something. The announcer even said 'Oh, the humanity!' like with the real Hindenburg."

Bud grinned, though he was actually thinking about his harmonica—he must've left it in the freezer when he'd gone for a bowl of vanilla-bean ice cream.

And even though he knew he was in trouble over the glass, it wasn't the first time, and he knew he would survive, especially with a stomach full of enchiladas.

He just hoped his wife wouldn't insist he go back to wearing those dang suspenders.

17

Bud figured it was a good thing they were having Frosty and Eileen's wedding rehearsal in the back yard, as that way no one would know he'd forgotten all about it. And to be honest, he'd also completely forgotten about the wedding, which was going to be held at the flagstone bandstand in the park the coming weekend.

Eldon would be the master of ceremonies, and Howie would provide the music. Eileen had chosen Maureen to be her maid of honor, and interestingly enough, since Eldon was officiating and couldn't play the part, Frosty had chosen Wilma Jean to be his best man, even though Eldon had told him one can't have a woman as a best man, as it bent tradition too much, not to mention definitions.

Wilma Jean had said it was fine with her, as long as she didn't have to dress the part, and she had then added that since most everyone in Frosty and Eileen's age cohort had already passed on and there was no one left to ask, who was to say that the old way didn't include women as best men? Besides, she was all for equality and would also back any man who wanted to be a maid of honor because it was good to be flexible in life.

Bud would be officiating the ceremony in his sheriff's uniform, and Frosty and Eileen had written their own vows, which everyone was eager to hear. Bud wasn't sure why the ceremony needed both him and Eldon to officiate, but he suspected it was Frosty's way of forcing Eldon to participate, since he'd refused to be his best man.

They had finished dinner, which had included a little wine, and it was time to get on with the rehearsal, so everyone gathered in the back yard, including the dogs, who were all excited, sensing that something unusual was in the air. Even little dachshund Pierre, who always grabbed onto Bud's pant leg and wouldn't let go, was instead running around with a large stuffed toy squirrel in his mouth.

Howie now plugged in his guitar amp and began playing "Here Comes the Bride" as Eileen walked across the yard with Maureen, followed by Frosty and Wilma Jean. Bud had no idea what a real wedding should be like, since the last one he'd attended was some years ago (his own), and he was beginning to get the idea that everyone was just making it all up as they went.

They reached the pretend stage, which was at the edge of Wilma Jean's rose garden, and Eldon came forward, taking the pretend microphone, saying, "Dearly beloved, we are gathered together today on this sad occasion to say goodbye to our dear friend Frosty, who will soon pass into another realm, one inaccessible to his old pals who used to run around with him at a moment's notice. From now on, he will live in the land of 'I have to check with my wife.'"

Eileen, looking irritated, said, "Eldon!" while Frosty tried to hide a grin.

Eldon then said, "What I meant to say is, dearly beloved, we are gathered together today on this happy occasion to welcome a new friend into the lives of the BOB-O's, the Bucket of Bolts Overlanders —our dear Eileen Jensen, who we promise to love and cherish, as long as she lets Frosty go whenever and wherever he wants."

Eldon then said as an aside to Frosty, "This is your last chance to bail, bud."

Wilma Jean, feeling a bit defensive of Frosty since she was his best man, said sternly, "Very funny, Eldon, but if you do this at the real ceremony, you won't be eating biscuits and gravy in my cafe."

"Alright, alright," Eldon replied, acting defeated, though Bud suspected he had other tricks up his sleeve. "If anyone besides me objects to this union, well, too bad, 'cause it's too late. Now, Sheriff Shumway will come up and make sure the marriage vows are legal."

Bud took the pretend microphone from Eldon, saying, "Friends, we now ask those who wish to be married to come forward." He then added, "Is that what I'm supposed to say?"

Frosty and Eileen walked up to Bud, each holding a small piece of paper as Bud asked, "Who's supposed to go first?"

Eileen waited for Frosty to offer, then said, "I will."

Reading from her paper, she said, "I, Eileen Jensen, take you, Frosty Merriott, to be my husband, to have and to hold from this day forward, for better, for worse, for richer, for poorer, in sickness and in health, to love and to cherish, until death do we part or you turn into a zombie, or worse yet, run off with Eldon."

She paused, then added, "But when I say, 'I do,' I don't necessarily mean the dishes. And I promise to love you, honor you, but not obey. But I do promise to keep you supplied with those yummy snickerdoodles you love more than me."

Frosty, grinning, said, "Ditto on all that, except I also promise to open jars for you, and I promise to let you win at Monopoly. I promise to try new things to eat, even though I know I won't like them, and I vow to stand by your side and to never tire of your wonderful snickerdoodles."

Bud grinned, then said, "I now pronounce you husband and wife, and you can kiss." He paused, then asked, "Where does the ring part come in?"

"Oh good Lord," Wilma Jean laughed. "This is going to be a wedding like none other. And you all know we're having a big buffet for everyone afterwards. Where are you guys going for your honeymoon?"

Frosty looked at Eileen, who replied, "I think we're going to go stay at the Super 8 in Salt Lake and do some shopping."

Eldon said in mock disgust, "I tried to get them to go camping in the backcountry with me. I told them I would supply them, then leave them alone, camp over the hill a ways."

Now Frosty said, "I think we're going to stay home and get some rest and eat cookies." He laughed, then added, "But we'll probably go on up to Salt Lake for a day or two after that."

Howie said, "After the vows, I play the Hawaiian Wedding Song, as that's what Eileen requested, but I still need to practice it some more."

"You should be playing Chained Melody. You know, the one by the Righteous Brothers," Eldon replied.

"I thought it was Unchained Melody," Howie said.

"Not anymore," Eldon said.

Wilma Jean said, "Let's go inside for dessert. Maureen made a pineapple upside-down cake that looks delicious. We can come back out and watch the sunset."

Bud waited until everyone had gone inside, threw the ball for Lindie for a bit, then went on in to get a bowl of vanilla-bean ice cream and retrieve his harmonica. He was glad it had been located and hoped the reeds had been dry when he'd left it there and hadn't frozen.

It had been a long day, and even though it had been mostly enjoyable, he just couldn't get rid of the nagging feeling that a crime could be in the making and the person who could potentially be the subject of said crime could also be the one who had sent him that cryptic letter.

If so, he had no idea what to do to prevent it. Maybe he should have paid attention to the part that said "no sleuthing permitted" and gone on with things, because he sure wasn't doing anything productive in that department as it was.

Back outside, he sat in a wicker chair and gave the dogs each a bite of ice cream, then, hearing the others laughing as they came back out, promised himself to try to enjoy the evening.

18

Bud sat tapping his fingers on his desktop while Howie sat in his usual chair across from Bud, casually flipping through a *Lost Treasure* magazine.

He was patiently waiting for the woman who'd put him on hold to return and was about ready to give up when she said, "I'm sorry Sheriff, but the coroner is out for a week as his wife's having surgery. They had to go to a special hospital in California. He did leave a note saying he was able to do the autopsy but didn't have time to write the report and would finish and get in touch with you when he got back. Is there anything else I can help you with?"

Bud sighed. It looked like he wouldn't have any news on what Ted had died from for awhile, which also meant he still had no idea if a crime had been committed or not. He guessed he'd have to continue to assume one had and keep on with his investigation.

"If you talk to him, give him my best," Bud replied. "And you have a good day."

Hanging up the phone, he took his harmonica from his pocket and started playing his old standby, *Red River Valley*. He was again wearing the suspenders, as per Wilma Jean's orders, but he preferred fiddling with the harmonica to the sting he inevitably got when he fiddled with them.

"Doesn't sound like you had any luck," Howie said, looking up from his magazine. "How are you supposed to investigate a crime if you don't even know if one's been committed?"

"Exactly," Bud answered. "I was just wondering the same thing myself."

Howie, looking alarmed, said, "Say, Bud, did you know there's a giant insect not too far above your head?"

Bud turned, looking at a praying mantis hanging from the window blinds.

"Oh, that's Jerry. I've been meaning to take him out to some place green, but I keep getting sidetracked. Let me get something to put him in, and we can do it now. He's probably getting pretty hungry."

"Jerry?" Howie asked. "I didn't know you had a pet praying mantis, Sheriff. Kind of unusual."

"He's not really my pet, Howie. He just showed up yesterday."

Howie continued. "How do you know it's not a she? And it sounds to me like you've kind of bonded with him, naming him and all. You know, Bud, I believe humans will bond with anything—literally anything. We're worse than baby ducklings. Do you still have that pencil stub in your desk drawer?"

Bud handed Howie what was left of a pencil.

"OK, Sheriff. See this little pencil? His name is Doodles—Little Doodles. Little Doodles here was once a nice tall fellow, strong and spiffy, called Mr. Woody, but he's been ground down and all used up by us humans, poor little fella."

"OK," Bud grinned.

"What kind of future does Little Doodles have now, Bud? What does a poor pencil stub like Little Doodles have to look forward to? He has no family to take care of him, no retirement pension, nothing. He's probably depressed from being in that dark drawer all the time, can't ever get out, nobody cares, forgotten."

As Howie was asking the question, he broke the pencil in two, and Bud instinctively flinched.

"See? You felt it when I broke him in two. You felt bad for Little Doodles. You bonded with him and felt his pain. You bonded with a *pencil*, Sheriff. I rest my case."

Bud laughed, saying, "Howie, you missed your calling. You should've been a prosecuting attorney. But I flinched because breaking a short stubby pencil like that can hurt your hands."

Howie brushed the splinters and graphite into a trash can, saying, "Maybe I should've named him Stubby. But poor Little Doodles has now been freed, even if broken. He will go on the journey of a lifetime to the town dump, where he'll meet others like him, his compadres. Who knows, he may meet up with a spiral notepad and write a book..."

"Howie, we need to get going before someone calls and I get sidetracked again," Bud said.

"Oh, right. I got a little carried away there, Sheriff. I've been spending too much time reading kids' books to Malcolm."

"Howie, Little Doodles would probably be a real hit at the grade school."

"Nah, they wouldn't even know what the story was about. They all use electronic tablets these days. OK, let's go, Sheriff."

Bud caught the mantis, using his lunchbox as a trap. He carefully closed the lid and they were soon on their way in the Sheriff's Land Cruiser.

"Where should I take him, Mayor?" Bud asked.

"How about the Melon View? Jerry would be happy in the gardens out there and not as likely to get run over, and Mollie might be serving tea or something good she'll share with us."

"Sounds like you're bonding with Jerry, too," Bud laughed, heading for the B&B.

As they pulled into the big circular drive, Bud could see several artists coming out the door, carrying easels and daypacks.

"This would be a good time for me to interview the couple who found the body, Howie, assuming they're still here. Would you mind finding Jerry a good home while I go find them?"

"Sure," Howie replied. "Say, Sheriff, did you ever find anything of interest on that drone camera?"

"It doesn't work. I think it got damaged when the drone crashed, though I was able to get the SD card out of it. But I still don't have a card reader, so I ordered one first thing this morning. I had it sent overnight."

"Should be interesting," Howie replied, taking Bud's lunchbox and heading for Molly's flower gardens.

Molly greeted Bud with surprise, then immediately said in a low voice, "Bud, you have to come see this. I didn't know whether to call you or not. When Kate saw it, she started crying, and Charles was also upset. I swear, that woman seems to be a walking drama troupe all by herself."

Molly led Bud to the easel, pointing at the place on the canvas where the Datura and hawkmoth had been. The hawkmoth was now painted over and replaced by one lying dead on the ground, feet up and its proboscis hanging out of its mouth.

"Isn't that the weirdest thing?" She asked. "And it looks like the same artist did it, the same style. Why would someone do this?"

"They should've painted little x's over its eyes," Bud mused, then added, "Just kidding. It *is* strange."

Molly said, "It almost seems as if someone's trying to get a message across, though what it would be is beyond me."

"I don't know," Bud replied. "Someone could just be messing around. Maybe they have a weird sense of humor."

Molly suddenly gasped. "Oh my gosh, Bud, I just made the strangest connection! That guy Hawk, he goes out of his way to not talk to anyone, he sent me an email this morning, asking to stay a few more days. Bud, his name is Hawk, and his avatar was a hawkmoth. Do you suppose this is someone's way of saying they're going to murder him?"

Bud replied, "Molly, that's pretty good sleuthing. I don't know—it could just be a coincidence. I'm not making any sense of a bunch of things right now, but it's something to think about. But are Kate and

Charles still here? I'd like to talk with them if they are, maybe back in the kitchen or somewhere private."

"I'll go up and see," Molly replied. "But I forgot to tell you that yesterday I made a big plate of finger sandwiches, left them in the kitchen while I watered the plants, and when I came back they were gone. Something fishy's going on, Bud."

She went up the stairs and soon returned, the couple following, then led everyone into the kitchen. Howie followed them in, having returned from releasing the praying mantis.

Eyeing the lunch box, Molly said, "We don't serve lunch here, Mayor. But I can offer coffee to whoever wants some. Have a seat."

They all sat around the country kitchen table as Molly brought a carafe of coffee, cups, and some cream. She disappeared for a moment, then brought a coffee cake and plates, along with a small bowl of ice cream for Bud.

"For your coffee," she smiled, then left.

As they all helped themselves to everything, Bud said, "I don't mean to take much of your time, folks, but I just have a few questions for you about when you were out in Black Dragon Canyon, if you don't mind."

Charles nodded amicably, his mouth full of coffeecake, but Bud noted Kate seemed nervous.

He continued. "We did go out there, but the body wasn't where you had indicated it might be. Any ideas what could've gone on?"

"What?" Kate asked, surprised. "He was right where we said, unless someone moved him. We left him lying at the base of a rock. He was on his back looking as if he could be asleep. In fact, that's what we thought, until we realized he was dead."

She looked at Charles as if silently asking for his corroboration.

"Did you see anyone else out there?" Bud asked.

"We didn't see anyone else, and I personally think he had a heart attack," Charles said. "He really did look like he was asleep."

"Did you see an older guy, one with gray hair wearing coveralls?"

"No."

"And tell me again where you found him?" Bud asked.

Charles said patiently, "He was about a hundred feet past the petroglyph panel, on the right-hand side of the canyon."

Bud asked, "Black Dragon Canyon, right?"

Charles looked perplexed. "Did we say that? We weren't in Black Dragon. It was the small canyon near the freeway, the one with the arch. He wasn't all that far from the arch, actually."

"There's a petroglyph panel in there?" Bud asked.

"Yes, it's not as nice as the one in Black Dragon, though. It's small, like the one in the next canyon over called Petroglyph Canyon."

"But didn't you say it was in Black Dragon?" Bud asked. "Howie, you were there. Did you hear them say Black Dragon?"

"That's how I remember it," Howie said.

Charles shook his head in dismay. "I recall saying out *by* Black Dragon, not *in* Black Dragon. But I guess I could've been more precise. I'm not sure I actually said it was in the canyon with the arch. In my defense, I was very upset."

"Double Arch Canyon," Howie said.

Bud suddenly felt a strange sense of detachment, as if he was losing his bearings. He stood.

"Howie, we need to get going. Thanks for your time, folks."

"Where did they take the body, if I might ask?" Charles asked.

"It's in the funeral home up in Price. Is that important?" Bud asked.

"I'd like to get a death certificate, you know, for his kids and such back home," Charles replied.

"Right," Bud replied, now feeling like he might start floating, as if the Great Attractor was pulling him away. He was now at the back kitchen door, saying goodbye, Howie close behind.

As they got to the Cruiser, Bud said, "Howie, could you drive? I'm not feeling so good."

"Gee, Sheriff, I hope you're OK," Howie replied, taking the keys.

"Howie, I think we need to go back out there," Bud replied. "We either found the wrong body or Ted was moved to the cave by someone else after Charles and Kate found him."

He paused, sinking into the passenger seat, then added, "Either way, I feel like I made a colossal mistake by not getting more details. Maybe I need to go back to full-time melon farming."

Howie was quiet for a bit, then said, "Sheriff, you're doing fine. But I've been meaning to tell you—you might not want to bond too close with a praying mantis."

"Why not?"

"They're cannibals."

"Well," Bud replied. "I guess that's a little disturbing, but better than finding out they eat people."

They drove on back to the office, the only sound being the Land Cruiser's engine, Bud glad Howie couldn't also hear the wheels turning in his head.

19

Bud was home, kicked back in his big recliner, dogs sleeping at his feet and his laptop open in front of him. He'd unhooked the front part of the suspenders, throwing them over his shoulders, as they were pushing against his stomach and making him uncomfortable.

The SD card reader had arrived, and he was now looking through the photos from the drone. He was impressed by how good the resolution was, as well as how smoothly the drone moved, the mark of a good pilot.

It was interesting seeing the canyon from the drone's viewpoint, hovering over the very top of the rim, a perspective Bud had never seen before. He could understand how one might be attracted to that type of photography, for you could go wherever you wanted with virtually no effort except using your thumbs to operate the controls.

At one point, Ted had made the drone hover over a nice stand of orange globe mallow, and the color against the gold sandstone was as nice as any photo he'd seen.

The drone's SD card actually held several videos, and as the first one ended, Bud started the second, wondering if it might have anything of interest other than the canyon itself. He didn't really know what he might find, if anything, but he wanted to be thorough and make sure Ted hadn't recorded anything that might give a clue as to how he died.

The second video seemed to be just a repeat of the first, and as Bud watched, he wondered how he could've been so mistaken about where Charles and Kate had said to look for the body. He had an unsettled feeling that he should go back out there ASAP.

He'd wanted Howie to go out with him, but he had to work at the drive-in and was unavailable. Doc and Millie had gone up on the Swell to where her cafe had been to see how the ravens she used to feed were doing, and Wilma Jean was at the cafe.

He'd have to go on his own, and he figured he probably should stop by the cafe and get something to take to Scratch while he was at it. The old guy had been on his mind a lot, and he'd been intending to call Nancy over at the city to see if she had any ideas of how to help him out.

Still watching the video, deciding what to order, thinking he might as well get himself some lunch while he was at it—something suddenly seemed out of place, just a brief glimpse of odd colors.

He rewound the video a few seconds and sure enough, it had briefly captured two blotches of color down on the canyon floor— one deep blue and one with red-and-yellow stripes. Because it was such a high view, it was impossible to make out what they were.

He now thought of the photo he'd downloaded from Ted's camera and the odd ghost-like colors—this was the same thing, only now there was no doubt about the colors. He got up and got the camera, taking it out of its case.

He'd seen a filter on the lens but had thought nothing of it until now, but he was now thinking he might know what was going on. Taking the filter from its holder, he read the small letters along its rim —*Lee Pro Glass 3.0 ND*.

Just as he thought, it was a neutral density filter, a device used to reduce the intensity of light entering the camera. This gave a photographer the ability to make long exposures in bright conditions, and he knew it was the secret behind photos of dreamy waterfalls, as well as buttery-smooth water in lakes and streams. He'd thought of getting one, but since there weren't many waterfalls or streams around, it would probably go unused, and they were expensive.

He also knew that ND filters were used to make people disappear in popular tourist places like the Eiffel Tower. Since most people don't stand in one spot for more than a few seconds, one could use an ND filter for a really long exposure and the camera wouldn't show anyone unless someone stood in one spot the entire time, though people who were slow to move might cause a little ghosting on the photo.

Bingo! He knew he now had pretty solid evidence that Charles and Kate had indeed been in Black Dragon Canyon, in spite of saying they hadn't, and the photo's time stamp would show exactly when. Looking at it, it appeared to have been the day before they came into his office and said they'd found the body.

This was odd, but not as odd as saying they hadn't been in Black Dragon. They freely admitted to being in Double Arch Canyon, where they said they found the body. Was it because they'd actually found the body in Black Dragon and were trying to throw Bud off? Had they killed Ted and hid him in the cave? If so, why report anything to the sheriff in the first place? Or had they gone into Black Dragon a different day for something else?

Leaning back, Bud decided to go ahead and place his order, calling the cafe. Wilma Jean answered, and he told her he needed two sack lunches and would be there in a bit, as he was going to Black Dragon, and if she had some extra scraps for Lindie, to put them in also.

He now turned back to the drone images, watching the third video. At first, it seemed to be yet more of the same, but soon the drone was hovering in place, the camera directed at something happening on the canyon floor.

It was difficult at first to make out what was going on, but as the drone pilot, who Bud figured must be Ted, lowered the drone, it became obvious someone was digging a hole in the sand while another someone stood nearby. Bud could now easily make out Kate and Charles, Kate standing near some sort of black bag and a long slim box while Charles dug.

Charles would stop occasionally to rest while Kate dabbed her eyes as if crying. Bud thought back to what Molly had said about her being her own one-woman drama troupe. It appeared they were ready to bury something or maybe someone.

Sure enough, the hole dug, they carefully lifted the box into it, then placed the black bag on top of it. Charles then set something small in the grave and began backfilling it while Kate stood by, again dabbing her eyes. They seemed unaware of the drone overhead, and Bud knew some of the newer drones were very quiet.

Once the hole was filled, they dragged some pieces of wood and rocks onto it, as if trying to make it look natural, then Kate picked some nearby lupine and placed it on what Bud knew had to be a grave.

All of a sudden, it appeared that they realized the drone was filming them, and they began throwing rocks at it. One must have struck it, for the video now became erratic as the drone tried to stay aloft, eventually crashing into some nearby rabbitbrush.

Bud could see the rotors were still turning from their shadows, and it appeared that the drone was jerking around in a circle, as if one of the rotors was broken. The drone continued spinning, then finally stopped, the video fading to black. He thought of how Scratch had said he'd cut his hand trying to stop the drone, yet there was no indication of any such thing.

He shut down his laptop, taking the dogs out into the back yard for a minute before he headed in to pick up his order from the cafe.

As he stood there, he wondered what the couple had buried and why they had wanted to keep it a secret. Had they killed Ted for filming them digging the grave? And what in hellsbells was going on with them saying they'd found a body in Double Arch Canyon? Was it a ruse to divert him from looking in Black Dragon? And why did they want a death certificate? Wasn't it good enough to inform Ted's wife Rachael of his death and let her get the certificate, since she was the one who would be dealing with his body? Or did Ted have family back in Tahoe?

Bud gave Hoppie and Pierre some biscuits, then hurried Lindie out the door so they wouldn't notice they were being left behind. As he closed the kitchen door behind him, he felt something pulling him back.

Puzzled at finding himself bound up and unable to move forward, he reached back and opened the door behind him, whereupon he felt the sting of a suspender smacking him on the back. He groaned— he'd forgotten to hitch them back up, and one had caught in the door.

Trying to clip them back onto the back of his pants, he realized he couldn't quite reach, so he was forced to unzip his cotton khakis and pull them down partway past his Scooby Do boxers and twist them around.

As he stood there with his pants half down, Old Man Green drove by in his old pickup and started honking and waving.

Suspenders finally back on, Bud sighed, feeling it was probably a portent of what was to come. Everything felt in disarray, and he knew he had no choice but to head back out to Black Dragon Canyon, where it was very likely he'd end up having to dig up what appeared to be a grave, assuming the canyon hadn't again been locked up.

20

Bud stood in front of the Black Dragon petroglyph, Lindie quietly at his side, wondering again how anyone could make out a dragon from what looked to him like a bird, but he knew he wasn't well-known for having a wild imagination—that was more Howie's forte.

Not far away stood a tall ghost-like figure wearing a shroud with vertical stripes that ended just above two thin stick-like legs and feet. It had no arms and its head was round like a coconut.

At the base of the panel a clump of Datura was starting to open its ethereal white blooms to welcome the cool evening, when the hawk-moths would arrive to pollinate it.

Bud usually enjoyed coming into the canyon, but today he felt a sense of detachment, and the Datura and petroglyph panel gave him a feeling of uneasiness, though he had no idea why. Maybe it reminded him of the strange progression of the painting at the Melon View B&B, with its Datura and now-dead hawkmoth.

He was tired, for he'd just walked the entire length of both Double Arch and Petroglyph canyons, looking for any evidence of a body, with no success. And he wasn't done, for now he needed to find the gravesite he'd seen on the drone's SD card.

Wondering where Scratch was, Bud began slowly walking down

the canyon to the place where the drone video had shown Charles and Kate burying something. He carried a small shovel and several evidence bags, but he suspected what was buried would need something larger, like a body bag.

He hadn't been able to make out what they'd buried, but from the size of the bag, it looked like a small person, maybe a child. He cringed—what if they'd not only murdered Ted, but had killed some innocent child? Or maybe they'd killed Ted because he'd seen them kill the child? Could it really be possible?

They didn't actually seem like the type, especially given the way they were worried about their dogs being cared for in their absence, but he knew people could be surprising.

He'd been able to pinpoint pretty closely where the grave was, for the drone showed it right under a large tiger wall, one down the canyon a ways from the Black Dragon Cave. Bud had seen it before in his wanderings, and he knew it was just a short walk away.

He knew that tiger walls were somewhat common in the canyons, places where desert varnish had created dark stripes on the lighter sandstone. The varnish was made of black streaks of manganese and iron oxide carried down the wall by runoff. Bud knew that when river rafters came upon such walls they were known to stop and kiss them, supposedly guaranteeing a safe trip.

Bud was soon at the big wall, and he began walking back and forth to pinpoint the disturbed area. It didn't take long, and he knew it was the right spot by the bunch of now-wilted lupine laid at what looked to be the head of a small grave.

His sense of detachment was gone, replaced by a feeling of despair. He had no desire to dig up a grave. It was a job he needed to hand off to the experts—the Utah State Bureau of Investigation.

As he leaned on the shovel, he noticed Lindie digging madly at the foot of the grave. Before he could tell her to stop, she'd unearthed some kind of round plastic object.

Telling her to drop it, Bud walked over and picked it up. It was about the size of a large donut and even had a hole in the middle, but it was green and yellow with two tortured-looking eyes painted on the top and a sad-looking mouth on the bottom.

Bud could make out some kind of writing, even though it was covered in dirt. It read: *Gogh-Nuts. Inedible Joy.*

Puzzled, he stuck it in his pocket where Lindie couldn't chew it up, then again leaned on his shovel. Reluctant to begin digging, he wondered if it hadn't been a toy that they'd buried with the child.

Thinking of the Van Gogh reference, he thought of Charles' Van Gogh t-shirt. It appeared the artist was a Van Gogh fan—had he been the one who sent him the letter signed Vinnie? And what were Gogh-Nuts? Was it some kind of child's teething ring? After all, it did have what looked liked chew marks on it. But did teething children have any teeth to leave such marks with?

Now he felt disheartened and wanted nothing more than to go home. The canyon suddenly felt cold and lonely, even though it was a beautiful sunny spring day.

As he picked up the shovel to leave, he was startled to hear a scratchy voice ask: "Did you bring me anything?"

It was Scratch! Glad to see him, Bud said, "Walk back to my rig with me and I'll give you the sack lunch I brought. But do you know anything about this?" He nodded at the grave.

Scratch looked puzzled, saying, "It looks like a grave, and a fresh one at that. But this is the first I've seen it. I need to put that lock back on the gate, Sheriff. This is pushing it. I thought tourists were bad enough, but now people are burying their dogs in here."

"Dogs? How do you know it's a dog?" Bud asked.

"From the size of it. Pretty obvious."

"It could be a child," Bud replied.

"That would be even worse. Is a child missing?"

"Not that I know of," Bud replied. "But Scratch, when we talked earlier, you said something about people pushing each other around. Was that here or over in Double Arch?"

"Double Arch."

"You're sure?"

"Positive, Sheriff. But what's this all about?"

"Just some stuff going on, Scratch. I'm not really at liberty to talk about it."

"This is my home, Sheriff," Scratch entreated. "I need to know what's going on. What if something was happening in your living room but I wouldn't tell you?"

"If something was going on in my living room I would already know about it," Bud replied.

Scratch sat on a nearby rock, petting Lindie.

"Sheriff," he said. "Why don't you arrest me and throw me in jail?"

Surprised, Bud replied, "Did you break the law?"

"No, but I could. I'm tired of trying to survive out here. At least I'd get three squares every day in jail."

"Did the Great Attractor tell you to leave?" Bud asked.

Scratch replied, "He doesn't care. If he did, I wouldn't be in this pickle in the first place. Once I get out of here, he can take a hike."

"Don't you mean *It*?"

"Right, with a capital I. I want to move into the Zone of Avoidance where It can't see me."

"Scratch, I don't even have a jail. It's over in Castle Dale, the county seat. All I have is a small temporary cell."

"Well, that takes care of that," Scratch said, disappointed. "You know, they say life gets more precious the older you get, but if you're hungry and thirsty and cold all the time, you kind of lose interest. I don't know how much more sand I have in my hourglass, but I know it's not gonna be much if I stay out here."

Bud sighed. "I've been trying to get ahold of the city to see if there's anything they can help you with. But tell you what. We have a little matter going on back in town that we need some help with. Maybe I could hire you on for a few hours a day, enough to get discount meals at my wife's cafe."

"Your wife owns a cafe? How lucky can a man get?"

"And I have an idea about a room, but I need to check on things first. It's not going to be anything you can count on long term, though, I can assure you of that, but maybe it can help you get back on your feet. I really do think you'll qualify for assistance if we can get you with the right people."

"I don't want to be a charity case, Sheriff. Well, actually, to be honest with you, I *would* like to be a charity case—retired and not having to work since I'm not getting any younger, but I'm willing to do what it takes. I guess I could manage to work a few hours a day."

They were at the Land Cruiser, and Bud opened the back door for Lindie and the front for Scratch, then handed him the sack lunch, wondering what he was getting himself into.

When they reached the gate, Scratch got out and opened it, and they headed for Green River, Bud glad to be leaving the mysteries of Black Dragon behind.

21

Bud had taken Scratch to the Green River Thrift Store and bought him a set of clothing and some shoes, then dropped him off at the Robber's Roost Motel, where he could clean up and spend the night. Bud had told him to go to the Melon Rind for dinner and also for breakfast the following day, where he would meet him.

Since Scratch didn't seem to trust that the cafe would serve him, Bud had written a note saying to feed him and the sheriff's office would pay for it. In reality, Bud knew he and Wilma Jean would foot the cost, not that it would amount to much. It wouldn't be the first time they'd fed someone down on their luck, Bud mused.

Bud had stopped by his office just in time to get a call from the River Museum, saying someone had cut the blooms off all their day lilies, as well as branches off their flowering plum trees. And not long after that, he got a call from a woman over on Solomon Street saying big sections of her lilac bushes had been cut off.

Perplexed, he wondered who would want to steal flowers, especially in such quantity. Was it just plain vandalism, or did someone have a reason?

As he was ready to walk out the door, he got another call.

"Sheriff Shumway speaking."

"Sheriff, this is Rachael Henderson."

"Good to hear from you Rachael. How are you doing?" Bud asked.

"I guess I'm getting used to the idea of being a widow, but it's hard, especially knowing my husband was cheating on me."

"Are you sure about that? Ted seemed like a pretty nice guy to me, a straight shooter. I remember him doing our wedding portrait, and he and I have had some good photography conversations."

"Well, something was going on with him staying out at that B&B. I haven't been able to figure out exactly what, and I'm trying to forget it. But I'm calling to tell you there's a memorial service for him this afternoon. We didn't have much notice, as my daughter's helping me put it together, and she just got informed she has to get back to work. She's a nurse. But Sheriff, we'd like you to come. It's at the Community Church at one."

"I'd be honored, Rachael. Are you expecting a big crowd?"

"I think so. He knew everyone in town, and if you talk to anyone, be sure to invite them. But have you heard anything back from the coroner? I have his ashes here, and my daughter and I will be taking them out to his favorite spot after the service."

Bud replied, "I haven't heard anything back, but I'll let you know when I do. But where was Ted's favorite spot?"

"He loved Black Dragon Canyon. Ironic, I know, since he died there. And Bud, I can't help but wonder if it didn't have something to do with this affair he was having. Maybe she wanted him to leave me and he wouldn't."

"Do you know who it was?"

"No."

Rachael paused until Bud thought she may have hung up, then she continued, "I have my suspicions, but I'll keep them to myself."

Bud thought back at the scene at the Melon View B&B that had upset Molly, and he suspected he knew who her suspect was.

She continued, "I don't know who it was for sure, but if I ever find out...But Sheriff, I hope you can make it to the service."

"I'll be there," Bud promised. "And would that be a good time to return his camera and drone to you? I needed to keep them for awhile as possible evidence, but I no longer need them."

"That would be fine," Rachael replied. "Did you find anything of interest?"

"Nothing of any real importance. I'll see you later."

As he hung up, he remembered Charles asking about getting a death certificate for Ted's family. Did Rachael know Ted had relatives, assumedly in Tahoe? Was she even aware that he'd been married before? Had her tirade out at the Melon View really been intended for Kate, not Molly, as she suspected he was getting back with his ex-wife? Did she even know his ex was in town?

So many questions, ones he didn't feel at all comfortable asking, though he knew he would eventually have to if things progressed in that direction.

He now remembered that Charles' business card had said he was an insurance adjustor. Were they trying to collect on Ted's insurance? Since Kate was Ted's ex-wife, was she still somehow his beneficiary?

Bud locked the office door, and though he needed to go out to the River Museum and check out the mischief there, he first wanted to go out to the B&B and see if Doc was around. He'd thought of just calling him, but he wanted to check on Molly and see if everything was going OK.

He felt like he needed to talk to someone about everything going on, and Doc was as good of a sounding board as one could get. And maybe he could talk him and Howie into helping him go back out to exhume that grave.

As Bud pulled up in front of the B&B, he noticed a gray sedan with Nevada plates, just like the one he and Howie had seen when going into Black Dragon to recover Ted's body.

The door opened and, to Bud's surprise, the Invisible Man got out. Bud met him at the front door.

"Afternoon," he said. The man tried to duck inside after saying hello, but Bud casually held the door closed, his hand on the handle.

The man looked directly at Bud, then asked, "Are you doing your job, Sheriff?"

Surprised, Bud wasn't sure what to say. He replied, "I sure hope so. But why do you ask?"

The man, ignoring his question, continued. "Have you seen anything unusual?"

Bud chose his words carefully, now suspecting the man was working up to something.

"There's always something unusual going on around here. It's typical for Green River. But say, I've forgotten your name."

"Hawk Papillon."

"That's right. You're from Sego. I wasn't aware anyone still lived there."

"I don't live there, I'm *from* there," Hawk replied impatiently. "I need to go inside, if you'll excuse me."

Bud opened the door, following Hawk inside, asking, "Your parents lived in Sego? I've been up there a number of times. There's some great photography there with all those old buildings."

Hawk turned, saying, "I was born there, and my family left soon after. I'm a very private person, and where I live is no one's business. How do you know I'm from Sego?"

"Molly told me. But what's a social entrepreneur?"

Looking even more frustrated, Hawk replied, "She needs to mind her own business. A social entrepreneur is someone who starts a business for the greater good of humanity and not just for money. My contribution to society is to free us from deceit and expose those who would do anything for money. But I need to go now, Sheriff. Just continue to do your job. I've heard you're quite good at sleuthing."

"Thank you," Bud said. "And I hope your hand is healing up OK."

Looking surprised, Hawk said nothing and bounded up the stairs.

Before he even had time to think about what Hawk had said, Bud realized he still had the Gogh-Nut in his pocket. He took it out and put it on a nearby side table, just as Molly spied him.

"Bud! Come take a look at this!" She led him over to the canvas by the fireplace, adding, "And when Kate saw it, she about had a meltdown."

The canvas now had a beautiful blue sky with wispy clouds, a nicely done arch, and the beginning of some canyon walls. The Datura and hawkmoth were gone, and painted in their place was the body of a man lying on his back as if asleep, but assumedly dead.

"They need to paint x's on his eyes to show he's dead," Bud said.

A voice behind them said, "But maybe he really *is* just sleeping."

Bud turned to see Doc, who added, "You need to do some more sleuthing, Sheriff. Maybe I can help."

22

Bud sat at the end of the last row in the church in case he needed to leave quickly, as he was on duty. He had his phone's ringer set to vibrate, and that way, he could leave without causing too much of a commotion.

Looking around, he tried to recall the last time he'd been in the Community Church, and he thought maybe it was when they'd held the last community potluck. He wasn't much for tradition, but he knew services like the one they were having today to honor Ted Henderson's life were important to some people for comfort and closure. He'd told Rachael he'd be here, so here he was.

It looked like a lot of other people had come, Bud noted, maybe even half the town. He knew that Ted had taken a lot of Green Riverites' portraits, as well as those of most of the school kids.

Wilma Jean had closed the cafe for a few hours, putting a sign on the door telling people about the service, but he didn't see any sign of her or Maureen or Millie, and he suspected they weren't here but were out enjoying a few hours off, probably sitting on the bungalow's back porch drinking tea.

And Molly could easily be with them, Bud noted, for he'd seen her put up a sign at the B&B saying she would be gone for the service.

He suspected that sign was why he was seeing a number of the B&B patrons, plein air artists who had known Ted before he died. He doubted very much if Molly would show up, given the insinuations Rachael had made about her and Ted having an affair.

Bud was still trying to figure out the connection between Ted and the B&B and why he'd stayed there, but he'd long ago decided it had nothing to do with art, but was some reason to get away from home. He'd decided not to go too far down that rabbit hole as it was all over and done with, now that Ted was gone.

Bud smiled as Doc, who was sitting next to him, tried to look solemn while surveying the crowd like an anthropologist deep in the Amazon. He was wearing a somewhat-dated camel-colored jacket of Bud's, while Bud wore his nice wool Pendleton jacket, though he was wishing he hadn't, as he was already starting to feel the heat.

As Bud surveyed the church, he noted that a nice array of flowers decorated the stage, and he wondered where Rachael had found such a nice assortment, as Green River didn't have a florist. He decided her daughter had probably brought them from Salt Lake, but a closer look revealed lilacs, sprays of plum blossoms, and bouquets of day lilies. He set up straight, suspecting these were the missing flowers that had been called in. He'd have to ask Rachael after the service where she'd gotten them.

The service now began, with the pastor giving a prayer for the living, then beginning his eulogy for the dead. Bud now noted that Kate and Charles were a few rows ahead of him, which for some reason surprised him, given the big argument they'd had with Ted. They both looked drawn and tired.

Bud thought back—it was that argument that had started this whole escapade, ending with them going out to find Ted's body. He still had no idea what was going on and why they'd said they'd never been in Black Dragon Canyon, saying they'd found Ted's body in Double Arch.

Now Bud noticed someone sitting at the end of the row ahead of him and realized it was the Invisible Man. He made a note to himself to quit calling him that, as he knew he was going to mess up and do it to his face. His name was Hawk Papillon, Hawk Papillon, Hawk Papillon, he said quietly to himself, though it was kind of hard to pronounce.

He was getting warmer and warmer and was beginning to feel like his wool jacket had its own internal heat source, which it actually did—he, himself. He tried to pull it away a bit to cool off, catching one of his suspenders and accidentally snapping it and jumping. He could see Doc trying not to laugh, and he silently cussed a society that would not only create such things, but would actually condone and even encourage wearing them.

The pastor was now getting carried away and sermonizing, jumping on his chance to try to convert more souls to his church by scaring them with a little hellfire and damnation. Bud could see that Hawk seemed to be taking it all in, his eyebrows raised and a subtle smile on his face.

Bud was now beginning to feel like he was going to pass out from the heat, the pastor not helping any with his vivid descriptions of fire and brimstone. He figured he was going to have to get up and leave soon if things didn't start cooling off.

For some reason, he flashed back on Mark Twain's *The Adventures of Tom Sawyer*, which he'd read in high school. He recalled the scene where the town was mourning Huck and Tom Sawyer and Joe Harper, thinking they were dead, all while the boys listened in on their own funeral service.

Bud recalled how everyone was in deep mourning, the entire church breaking down in tears, wondering how they could have overlooked the goodness in the boys. He then remembered how his teacher had said that Twain used humorous irony to show the hypocrisy of adult society, which only perceives the worth of its members once they've passed away.

Bud wondered if maybe he shouldn't plan his own funeral, mostly to prevent the kind of sermonizing he was currently listening to. He didn't figure it would take much time—he could just put a few photos he'd taken to some music—maybe something like *Ghost Riders in the Sky*, which he could even record himself on his harmonica. And once he did it, the best part was he'd never have to do it again.

Now Rachael was at the podium, reading a poem she'd written for Ted about what a good husband he'd been to her and a good dad to their daughter.

Bud could see that Kate was now crying, Charles trying to reassure her, and he could see Hawk watching them with what Bud took to be a mix of amusement and puzzlement.

Doc, also watching Hawk, whispered, "Schadenfreude or epicaricacy, Bud. Deriving pleasure from the misfortune of others."

"What's going on, Doc?" Bud whispered back, feeling like he was about to pass out.

"Let's go—you're white as a sheet," Doc replied, standing and taking Bud by the elbow and helping him up and out the door into the fresh air.

The last thing Bud remembered was Doc saying, "Let me help you get that coat off," and he was then out as cold as one could be on a hot day while wearing a wool jacket.

Bud woke on the steps outside of the church, Doc having pulled off the wool coat. The first thing he asked for was a bowl of vanilla-bean ice cream.

Doc immediately drove them to the Chow Down, where he got them each a vanilla shake. Bud figured it was one of the best shakes he'd ever had, especially since it had replaced having to shake hands with his constituents after the memorial service.

Feeling better, they went back to the church to get the Land Cruiser, and Bud headed for the office, where he could rest up and cool down, eventually going home and playing fetch with the dogs from the back porch of the bungalow, forgetting all about telling Rachael he'd stop by with Ted's camera gear.

23

It was the next morning, and Bud sat in the back booth of the Melon Rind Cafe, drinking coffee with Doc and listening to Howie and Scratch talk in the next booth. Scratch was wearing the clothes Bud had bought, and Bud couldn't help but think he looked like a completely different person, his long gray hair now clean and pulled back in a neat ponytail.

"I'm not an astronomy genius, I just find it all interesting," Howie was saying.

"But you seem to know all about the Great Attractor. Don't you worry about It killing us all if we ignore It?" Scratch asked.

"Scratch," Howie replied patiently, "Humankind hasn't known anything about it until the 1970s. That's when it was first found that there was something messing with the dark energy that causes the universe to expand, you know, from the Big Bang. If it was going to kill us, it would've done so by now. Actually, it *is* going to kill us, providing any of us are still around then."

"What do you mean?"

"The universe is expanding. Astronomers can see it through an increase in wavelength called the red shift, which tells them an object is traveling away. But certain objects aren't red shifting at the same rate as the rest of the universe, which leads scientists to believe there's some kind of gravitational force attracting them. The Great Attractor is thought to be at the gravitational center of the Laniakea Supercluster—a giant blob of which the Milky Way is but one galaxy. Mass causes gravitational pull, and the Great Attractor has to be very dense to cause that kind of pull. We're talking over 100,000 galaxies in the Supercluster. Over the course of billions of years, the Great Attractor has been pulling us and all the galaxies near us closer to it."

"It sounds kind of scary."

"It *will* be in billions and billions of years. Since all galaxies are clumping into greater and greater superclusters because of gravitational attraction, the universe may end in what astronomers are calling the Big Crunch, which could theoretically be followed by another Big Bang. But our sun's going to explode long before that—in a mere six or seven billion years."

"Something new to worry about, eh?" Scratch said with concern. "But the universe is kind of like a slinky going down a set of stairs, huh, Howie? It expands, then contracts, then expands, over and over."

"That's a good analogy in some ways," Howie replied. "Partly because the amount of matter stays the same, whether it's contracted or expanded. But how did you come about being a fan of the Great Attractor?"

Scratch shook his head. "I'm not—not at all. I was just minding my own business when this guy started coming into the canyon to take night photos. He offered me some hot chocolate one night, and we ended up talking about it. He's the one who told me about it, then I later had a vision that it was true."

"A vision?" Howie asked.

"I'd rather not talk about it," Scratch said, stirring his coffee. "Let's just say we got to be friends and every time he'd come out, we'd have some tea and talk around the campfire. We've both had lots of visions since then. He was one of those who was bringing me food when he came out. Probably the only reason I'm still alive."

"Does he still come out?" Howie asked, knowing that Ted had been taking night photos.

"No, he quit, and I don't want to talk about it," Scratch replied. He then said to Bud, "But we do need to talk about this job you have for me. I checked out of the motel and don't have any place to go."

"Right," Bud said, just as his phone rang.

"Yell-ow," he answered.

"Sheriff Shumway, this is Judy at the coroner's office in Price. The doctor called in, and I mentioned that you'd called earlier. He requested that I contact you and tell you the results of the autopsy. I assume you'll know who he's referring to?"

"I do," Bud replied.

"He is going to be held up for another week and can't get the report to you for awhile, but he said to go ahead and tell you the coroner's office has concluded its investigation and ruled the cause of death to be cardiovascular collapse. He had high levels of alkaloids in his body."

Bud paused, then said, "Wish him well for me, and thanks for relaying that information, It's very helpful."

Realizing everyone was listening in, he hung up and said, "Just a little report I've been waiting on. But let's all go on back out to the Melon View B&B. That's where your new job will be, Scratch."

"Do I have time to run across the street and get a cigar at the gas station?" Scratch asked. "Haven't had one in ages."

"Sure," Bud replied. "We'll wait for you here."

"Can I have an advance on my wages, Sheriff? I don't need much, just enough for a couple of cigars."

Bud knew they didn't sell cigars, but he wanted to have a moment alone with Doc and Howie. He took out his wallet and handed Scratch a ten-dollar bill, then after Scratch was gone, asked Doc, "What exactly is cardiovascular collapse? The coroner says that's what killed Ted, but let's keep that just between us. He also said he had high levels of alkaloids."

Doc looked surprised. "Cardiovascular collapse? It's basically a general term referring to loss of sufficient cerebral blood flow to maintain consciousness caused by acute dysfunction of the heart and/or peripheral vasculature."

"You sound like a textbook," Howie grinned.

"I've read my share," Doc replied. "But basically, it's when your heart can't maintain your blood flow. It can be caused by a number of things, though ventricular fibrillation is a common one. You get weak and dizzy and eventually you pass out and die. It takes only about 10 minutes from collapse to death."

"So that's what happened to Ted," Howie mused. "But what caused it?"

"Since the coroner said he also had high levels of alkaloids, my guess is he ate or drank something toxic. That would definitely cause cardiovascular collapse," Doc replied.

"His wife said he hadn't taken his meds," Bud said. "It sounds like he may have also had something else going on."

He could see Scratch coming back across the street from the gas station.

"No cigars," Scratch said.

"Keep it and just call it an advance," Bud said.

Scratch grinned. "I bought some jellybeans instead. But what's this job you have for me?"

"Well, assuming you agree to it, we need someone to help Molly, the manager of the Melon View B&B. She's pretty inundated by guests. Your job will be to do whatever she wants, which will probably include cleaning, doing laundry, and even some yard work."

"That sounds OK," Scratch said. "Maybe I can get a job with that Meals On Wheels thing you told me about if this doesn't work out."

Bud continued. "The garage out there has a workroom with a bathroom, and we're going to set you up with a bed and whatever you need, and Molly will provide you with meals as part of the deal. You can keep track of your hours, and we'll pay you for them. But we also need you to do some detective work."

Now Scratch looked doubtful. "I'm not too good at figuring things out. Will there be arrests and gunplay?"

Bud laughed. "I hope not. You'll be doing more in the realm of surveillance, seeing if you can figure out whoever's doing whatever, things like stealing flowers and food."

"Stealing flowers and food?" Scratch asked, incredulous. "I could understand stealing food if you're starving, but flowers? Who steals flowers?"

"That's hopefully something you can figure out. And in the meantime, I'm going to be working on finding you a permanent place. But you'll have to watch your P's and Q's, as Molly runs a tight ship. She'll be your manager."

"I've never had a manager," Scratch replied as they all got into Bud's Land Cruiser. "Just bosses. But it's OK, as long as she doesn't display favoritism."

"Well, since you'll be her only employee, I don't think you need to worry about that," Bud replied, starting the vehicle. "But let's go on out and get everything settled, then me and Doc and Howie need to get going. I have a job for them, assuming they agree to it."

Doc and Howie both looked concerned, but Bud ignored them and turned on the radio, KOAL up in Price. *When It's Springtime in the Rockies* was playing, that old song Gene Autry had made popular way back in the 1930s.

Bud remembered his grandmother singing that song to him, and he wondered if it wasn't maybe something he could learn on his harmonica, thinking maybe it was time to take his playing to a new level, since he obviously wasn't able to do so with his sleuthing abilities.

And he knew if Doc and Howie didn't agree to help him dig up that grave, he wasn't sure what he would do next, for he didn't think he had it in him to do it alone.

24

"Doc, is it possible to tell what kind of ashes we have here?"

Bud, Doc, and Howie were in Black Dragon Canyon, Bud holding a small gray ceramic urn that held what looked to be someone's ashes.

"Only if a few bone fragments made it through the cremation. If so, a lab can extract enough DNA to tell if they're human or not."

The trio had dug up the small grave, but all they'd found, to their relief, was the urn with its tight-fitting lid and a black plastic bag that held an assortment of stuffed animals, along with a small fuzzy blue blanket. Underneath it all they'd also found a long lightweight rectangular box wrapped in tape and plastic.

Leaning on a shovel and impatient to get going, Howie asked, "What now, Sheriff? Do you think these could be a child's toys? What should we do with them?"

"I don't really know, Howie," Bud replied. "If this is a child, we need to take everything as evidence."

He thought of the strange Gogh-Nut Lindie had found. It had probably slipped from the bag and wasn't buried very deep in order for her to be able to dig it up so quickly. He wondered again if it was some kind of teething ring.

"Let's bag this all up, fill in the grave, and get on back," Bud said, now hearing people talking over by the petroglyphs and suspecting tourists were in the canyon.

After filling in the grave, Bud carried the urn, while Doc and Howie carried the black bag and package, which they all suspected was some kind of painting.

Walking down the canyon on their way to the Land Cruiser, they heard the drone of an oncoming airplane. Looking up, Bud could see it was pink, and he knew it was Wilma Jean.

What would she be doing out here, he wondered. Last he'd talked to her, she was planning on spending the day at the cafe, as they were as busy as usual.

The plane dipped lower and was now overhead. Bud waved, and the plane waggled its wings, then flew on over the canyon.

Now back on the road to Green River, they all rode along in silence, and Bud felt a sense of heaviness, as if they all were thinking of the ashes they'd found and what they could represent. In addition, Bud wondered if Wilma Jean had waggled her plane's wings to say hello or to indicate that she was in some kind of trouble.

Finally back in town, Bud dropped Howie off at his drive-in, then said, "Doc, I need to go take that drone and camera gear back to Ted's wife. I was supposed to do it after the memorial, but for obvious reasons didn't make it. Do you want to come along, or should I take you back to the B&B?"

"I'll go along, Sheriff. Never know when you might need a side-kick," Doc replied, grinning.

They were soon at Rachael's, and when she came to the door, Bud handed her the tripod, as well as a box with the drone and camera in it.

"Sorry I didn't get this to you at the memorial," he said. "But I had a little problem and had to leave early."

"I noticed you left. I hope everything's OK," she replied.

"I got a little overheated with all the fire and brimstone talk," Bud replied. "There were also a lot of warm bodies in the church, and it got to be a little too much for me."

"I was totally shocked at how many people came," Rachael said. "People I'd never even met, and after reading the autograph book, I noticed some were from Lake Tahoe. I'm beginning to think he had a secret life, Bud. Did you know anything about it?"

"No, not at all, Rachael. He seemed like a pretty straight up guy to me, not the type to have anything he should hide. Did you guys ever live in Tahoe?"

"No, we've both lived here since we were kids. But look at his camera! What in the world happened to it? He always took good care of his stuff."

"I don't know," Bud replied. "It almost looks like he dropped it on a rock or something. But Rachael, did Ted have any health problems?"

"Oh, no, he was healthy as an ox. He ate well and got lots of exercise out wandering around taking photos."

"But didn't you say he forgot his medicine when you called me worried about him?"

"Oh, that. Yes, he had arthritis, but it wasn't too bad if he stayed on his meds. But he'd just gone to the doctor up in Price for his annual checkup, and his heart was in good shape."

"Did he ever take any drugs?"

"Drugs? You mean like illegal stuff? Oh gosh no, not that I ever knew of. Why would you ask a question like that?"

"No real reason, just being thorough," Bud replied.

"Do you know what caused his death?" Rachael looked like she was about to start crying.

Bud, deciding not to mention the alkaloids, tried to reassure her. "The coroner said he had heart failure, basically. You know, none of us know for sure what's going to take us away, and even though the doctor said he was healthy, he may have missed something."

"I would've never guessed that."

"Well, he was a great guy," Bud said lamely, now just wanting to go.

"I wish I knew why he'd gone and stayed at that B&B," Rachael said. "It really shakes my ability to think I know what's going on with people. I thought I knew my own husband so well..."

"I'm sure there was a good explanation," Bud replied. "I do know that Molly, the manager, is happily married, Rachael. But if I ever hear anything, you'll be the first to know."

"Thank you," she replied.

"But Rachael, one last thing," Bud continued. "Where did you get the flowers for his service?"

"You'll have to talk to my daughter. She arranged all that. Would you like her number?"

Rachael gave Bud her daughter's number, they said their good-byes, and Bud got back into the Land Cruiser, where Doc waited.

Bud sat for a moment, thinking.

"Anything of interest?" Doc asked.

"She said he'd just had a checkup and his heart was fine," Bud replied. "And he didn't do drugs."

"Are you thinking of the alkaloids?" Doc asked.

"Yes. Remember that comment Scratch made about them both having visions? That could be from taking drugs. Scratch said he had a vision about the Great Attractor, and I don't really think he was sent here by some bogus gravitational deity, Doc. It almost seems as if they were out there enjoying the night sky a little too much. And Scratch mentioned they were drinking tea. Scratch couldn't afford drugs, though Ted maybe could, but he just doesn't seem the type. What could they be drinking out there that would give them visions?"

"Maybe Brigham tea, Ephedra nevadensis, also known as Mormon tea. It sounds like it has ephedrine in it," Doc replied. "It grows all over the place. It can cause sudden cardiac death."

"Does it cause hallucinations?"

"Ephedrine is a stimulant, so maybe," Doc replied. "I'm really not sure. There could be something else out there, but that's the first that comes to mind."

"I have a feeling something like that was going on, Doc. But I can't figure out the role Kate and Charles had in all this. Scratch said he saw them push someone off a large rock, and they came into my office and said they found Ted, and he was dead. It's all very perplexing. But we need to get this stuff from the grave to my office. I'm wondering what's in that package that's all wrapped up."

"I think it's some kind of painting," Doc replied. "But I never thought I'd be a grave robber. And by definition, it's illegal, Sheriff. Grave *robber*."

"So when does grave robbing become archaeology?" Bud asked.

Doc thought for a moment, then said, "Desperate scallywags are grave robbers. Educated people with grants and PhDs are archaeologists."

Bud replied, "I think it has more to do with hoping to find black-market loot versus finding scientific evidence, Doc. Besides, archaeologists don't usually excavate recent burials, as far as I know."

"Forensic archaeologists might," Doc replied.

Bud paused, then asked, "Doc, what did you mean by saying maybe that guy in the painting wasn't dead, but was sleeping?"

"I don't know, just something to think about, Sheriff," Doc replied. "But I sure could use a cup of coffee. Since we're here, can we run through Howie's Drive-In and get a coffee and sandwich?"

"*Mayor* Howie's Drive-In," Bud laughed, turning into the drive-through lane and stopping in front of the speaker. A tinny voice asked, "Mayor Howie, can I take your order?"

Doc replied, "Two ribbon cuttings with a side of administrative nonsense, one lighting of the town's Christmas tree, three honor citations for do-gooders, and a bunch of first pitches at Little League games. All to go."

Howie laughed. "You rascals have to come inside to eat. As Mayor, I can't serve ne'er do wells at the drive through. You might run over someone while eating and driving. Come on inside and lunch is on me. I need to run a new idea by you—I'm thinking a dairy would be great. We grow lots of hay here."

Bud and Doc both shook their heads, then Bud parked the Land Cruiser, and they went inside.

25

After lunch at Howie's, Bud had taken Doc out to the B&B, for Millie had called saying she wanted her husband back to go play golf. As Doc got out of the vehicle, he said, "You know, Bud, long ago, when men cursed and beat the ground with sticks, it was called witchcraft, but now it's called golf."

Bud laughed at the thought. Now in his office, he was studying the text on his computer screen, which read:

Mormon tea is made from a plant, Ephedra nevadensis. The dried branches are boiled in water to make the tea. People use it as a beverage and as a medicine.

Be careful not to confuse Mormon tea (Ephedra nevadensis) with ephedra (Ephedra sinica and other ephedra species). Unlike these other plants, Mormon tea does not contain ephedrine, an unsafe stimulant. As a medicine, people use Mormon tea for colds and kidney disorders, as well as other conditions, but there is no good scientific evidence to support these uses.

He leaned back. If Scratch and Ted had been hallucinating, Doc was wrong—it wasn't from drinking Mormon tea. There had to be another reason. Maybe they were drinking alcohol, or better yet, maybe he was being presumptuous to take Scratch seriously, as he did seem to be a little half-cocked. But the coroner had said he'd found a high level of alkaloids.

Next, curious ever since Howie had called Hawk the Invisible Man, he did a search.

First published in 1897, The Invisible Man by H.G. Wells ranks as one of the most famous scientific fantasies ever written. Wells' years as a science student undoubtedly inspired a number of his early works, including this strikingly original novel. Set in turn-of-the-century England, the story focuses on Griffin, a scientist who has discovered the means to make himself invisible.

"I was invisible, and I was only just beginning to realize the extraordinary advantage my invisibility gave me. My head was already teeming with plans of all the wild and wonderful things I now had impunity to do."

Bud pondered how it would feel to be invisible and all the things one could do, like help themselves to free food. He'd read the book in high school, but now recalling the guy had abused his powers and things hadn't gone so well, he decided he'd rather stay visible, if ever given the choice.

He figured it was time to go home and take a break and check on the dogs.

Just then, his phone rang.

"Yell-ow," he answered.

It was Wilma Jean. He'd tried calling her several times once they'd gotten back into town, with no luck.

"Hi hon, are you trying to get ahold of me? Maureen said you called the cafe several times, and I have two messages on my cell phone. Is something important going on?"

Bud sighed in relief. "I was just wondering why you were out waggling over the canyons. I was kind of worried something was wrong, as you didn't mention going flying."

"I thought that was something bees do."

"What, waggle?"

"Yes, they do this waggle dance where they tell the others how to get to flowers. But since you asked, I've created a new job for myself. Sammy wanted me to come out to the airport and show off my plane to the RC club out there. He thought they might enjoy seeing the real deal. He's very proud of his paint job."

"Did they like it?" Bud asked.

"Oh did they ever. Hon, I'm making some good money giving them all sight-seeing flights. A dollar a minute each, and I can take up three passengers. Ain't that somethin'? I even took the blimp pilot up. Howie needs to ask me about economic development, 'cause I'm right in the middle of doing it."

"I thought the idea was to help the town's economy, not just your own," Bud teased.

"I will," she replied. "I'll end up spending it around town—you know, groceries, gas, that kind of thing."

"Well, it's not every day one gets to fly around in a pink Cessna," Bud replied. "But I'm on my way home for awhile. Are you still at the airport?"

"I have to get back to the cafe," she replied. "Take some hamburger from the freezer to thaw. I want to make a meatloaf for dinner."

They hung up, and Bud was standing to go when he remembered the sealed package from the grave. He normally would never forget something like that, but he figured his subconscious was trying to divert him, as he was finding the whole affair to be somewhat disconcerting.

He got it back out of the evidence safe and set it on his desk, then carefully began to pull off the tape, using his pocket knife.

It took some doing, as it was large and well-wrapped, but he finally had it to where he could stand it up and take a look.

Whistling, he felt a sense of awe, for he knew he was looking at a Van Gogh painting, and it had to be an original, for he could easily make out the brush strokes, as well as a few chips in the paint and even some minor cracks in the canvas. It was impressive, a landscape with a few white clouds set in a brooding blue sky, all over a field of greens and yellows.

His first instinct was to call Doc, but he knew doing so would be walking a thin line with Doc's wife, Millie, who probably was feeling somewhat deserted, even though she'd actually been hanging around with Wilma Jean and Maureen.

But he knew he was out of his element, knowing almost nothing about art, especially Van Gogh. But he did recognize Van Gogh's signature swirls in the clouds in the sky, as well as his bold use of color, and he knew the painting was probably worth a good sum of cash.

Sitting back down, he booted his computer back up and did a search on paintings by Van Gogh. He quickly recognized the one he had—it was called *Wheatfield Under Thunderclouds* and was oil on canvas and supposedly housed in the Van Gogh Museum in Amsterdam.

He read:

In the last weeks of his life, Van Gogh completed a number of impressive paintings of the wheatfields around Auvers. This outspread field under a dark sky is one of them. The elongated format of Wheatfields under Thunderclouds emphasizes the grandeur of the landscape, as does the simple composition: two horizontal planes.

Bud now did a search on sales of Van Gogh paintings and was shocked to find that some of his paintings had sold recently for over 100 million dollars, with an average of 30 million each.

Why wasn't this painting under glass or something, he wondered. It had simply been wrapped in paper and taped, almost as if someone had been in a hurry to hide it. It had to be a copy of the real one, he figured, yet the three-dimensional nature of the painting, including the thick strokes and flaws in the canvas, spoke to it being genuine.

He carefully wrapped it back in the paper and put it in the safe, then headed out the door. He really wanted to talk to Doc and see if he had any ideas about what was going on, but he realized he was on his own, which was technically as it should be, as he was the one getting paid to uphold the law and solve crimes.

As he headed out to the bungalow, he again mulled over the letter he'd received. It seemed like so long ago, with its ultimatum of no sleuthing allowed.

It had to be some kind of taunt, he figured, a way to gig him into doing that very thing. He thought again of how the Invisible Man had asked him when they'd met at the B&B if he was doing his job, then told Bud his own contribution to society was to free everyone from deceit and expose those who would do anything for money.

Had the Invisible Man written that letter? The way he'd asked Bud if he was doing any sleuthing had seemed to hold more under the surface than one might think—or was it just coincidence?

Why was the guy so hell-bent on not talking to anyone and covering himself from head to toe? What was he hiding? And who was painting the strange stuff on the canvas back at the Melon View? It had to be someone staying there, and it also had to be someone Charles and Kate knew, for she'd said she recognized the style. But why would that upset her so much?

Now back at the bungalow, Bud felt like he needed a nap, but the dogs were bouncing around, wanting to go somewhere. Maybe they all just needed to get out for awhile.

He'd take some hamburger from the freezer for dinner, make a thermos of coffee, grab his harmonica, camera, and some Barkie Biscuits, and head out into the Big Empty. He knew he could get away from everything out there and regain his balance and regenerate his energies for the next round, whatever that might bring.

He was soon in his FJ, the dogs half-hanging out the windows, heading out the River Road to the land of freedom and peace, where he would hide out, at least until he needed to go back that evening for the meatloaf dinner his wife had mentioned.

26

Bud and the dogs were hanging out watching the clouds, a good 10 miles from town along a narrow two-track road that eventually headed down toward the river, when he noted a black band in the far distance over the Swell. He made a mental note to be sure to check the weather when he got home, as it looked ominous. These spring storms could bring heavy snows without much warning, then the next day would be warm again, the snow melting.

Hoppie was sleeping in the shade, having just eaten his fill of biscuits, and Pierre was rooting around under a large rabbitbrush, looking for badgers or such, Bud figured.

Bud had been playing ball with Lindie until it occurred to him that perhaps she was bringing it back only because she thought he liked throwing it, not because she liked playing chase.

Stopping to ponder the thought, he sat on the FJ's bumper, again wondering if a storm were imminent. Maybe he should go back a little earlier than he'd planned, besides, meatloaf with mashed potatoes and gravy was starting to sound pretty good.

He pulled out his harmonica and began trying to play *Springtime in the Rockies*, fumbling the chords a bit, then finally putting it back in his pocket and humming the tune.

The song held a lot of fond memories for him, it being his Grandmother O'Connor's favorite tune, even though they never actually lived in the Rockies, being Utah bred and born.

He knew his grandfather loved fishing, and when the farm chores allowed, he and Bud's grandmother often took off for nearby Colorado, where they camped and fished to their heart's delight. Bud had been lucky enough to go with them occasionally, and he knew well the attraction to the high country with its ethereal peaks and graceful aspen trees.

He began softly singing.

> When it's springtime in the Rockies,
> I'll be coming back to you.
> Little sweetheart of the mountains,
> With your bonnie eyes of blue.
> Once again I'll say I love you,
> While the birds sing all the day.
> When it's springtime in the Rockies,
> In the Rockies far away.

Feeling somewhat poignant, he now began thinking about Ted and how he'd probably been enjoying the canyon country just like Bud was, no idea he would soon be gone forever.

Lindie, perhaps sensing Bud's feelings, came and put her head in his lap, looking up at him.

"You guys don't worry about such things, do you?" He asked. "You're lucky, as it's kind of a curse. You just live for the day." He thought of the seal on the letter he'd received—*Nothing in life is permanent.*

Wishing he'd brought a snack, he decided to go back home, now getting the dogs in the FJ. He sat in the front for a minute, watching a pair of pronghorn antelope on a nearby hillside, then reached to start the FJ just as something caught his eye.

Someone was walking down the road! He wondered why someone would be walking way out here, figuring they must be broken down or run out of gas and needed help.

They were soon close enough that he could make out a thin figure all bundled in dark clothing, including a black fedora with a white silk headband and a thick cream-colored scarf wrapped around their neck.

It was the Invisible Man, Hawk Papillon! How odd that he'd be walking out here, so far from town, and Bud couldn't help but again note his thick Groucho Marx eyebrows and mustache that almost looked comical. Molly was right, they had to be fake.

"Afternoon, Hawk," Bud said. "You need a ride?"

"It depends on where you're going," Hawk replied cryptically.

"Is your car out here? I can take you back to town or wherever you need to go."

"Can you take me back to my previous life?" Hawk asked.

"I don't understand," Bud said.

"My life before everything got so confusing."

"If I could, I'd take myself there, too," Bud replied. "Mine's gotten a little strange, too."

"Did it have anything to do with the plein air artists coming?" Hawk asked.

Bud thought for a minute, then said, "Well, yes, I guess it did."

"They're a bunch of thieves," Hawk advised. "Be careful." Seeing Bud's confusion, he added, "Not all of them, just a couple."

"Would that couple be Charles and Kate by any chance?" Bud asked.

"They're liars, too," Hawk said.

"Do they have any children? Would they kill anyone?" Bud asked, not sure where the conversation was going.

"No kids as far as I know, and I can't see them killing anyone. They're not all bad, you know, just greedy. Mostly Kate. It could just be her wanting revenge, since she didn't get everything she wanted when we divorced. But since he goes along with it, Charles is to blame, too."

"What did they do?" Bud asked.

"Like I said, they're thieves. Thieves steal things."

"What did they steal?"

"*You* of all people should know."

"Me?" Bud was incredulous. "How would I know?"

"You know."

Bud could see that the clouds above the Swell were moving in faster than he'd expected, dark swirling masses that reminded him of a Van Gogh painting.

"Do you know anything about Van Gogh?" Bud asked.

"More than I want to at this point," Hawk replied.

"I have a painting that could be by him."

"I know."

Wondering how Hawk knew, Bud said, "I need an expert to look at it. Would you be willing to come to my office and take a look?"

"I'm not an expert. What are you going to do with it?"

"I don't know."

Bud suddenly felt like he wasn't being prudent sharing this information and was regretting mentioning it. What if it was stolen and Hawk had something to do with it?

Bud asked, "Are you really just a tourist visiting?"

Hawk replied, "In some ways, yes, in other ways, no."

Now Hawk leaned on the FJ, closer to Bud, and Bud could see that his mustache and eyebrows were indeed cardboard.

"How do you keep your eyebrows and mustache from falling off?" Bud asked.

"They're glued."

"Who are you, really?" Bud asked.

"I could tell you, but it doesn't matter, as we've never met. I will say that I'm not who you think I am. I like looking like Groucho Marx, though, as it confuses people. But I'm actually the Invisible Man. You can't see me unless I cover up with clothing and hats and such."

Bud wondered how Hawk knew that he and Howie had called him that.

Hawk continued. "I'm invisible, and there are lots of wild and wonderful things I now have the impunity to do."

"That's from the book, isn't it?" Bud asked, now feeling like something was wrong, that maybe he was hallucinating. He snapped his suspenders, trying to see if he was awake, jumping from the sting.

Hawk laughed. "This isn't a dream. I'm real. You hang out in the desert long enough, and reality can get a bit tenuous. But I will say that you're more confused than normal. The answers are simple."

Bad asked, "Why were you guys at the memorial service? Did you know Ted?"

"No, none of us knew Ted. I was there to see if it was my *own* service, but it wasn't, though some thought it was. Just a mixup. Kind of like Huckleberry Finn and Tom Sawyer."

Bud was surprised that Hawk had also thought of Tom Sawyer in the context of the service.

Hawk continued. "There's an old saying that nobody ruins a good story like a witness. You have a witness, if you'll just listen to him. It might ruin your story, but in a revealing way, as it seems complicated, though it's actually not. You might want to think about that death certificate. But I'm going to keep walking. See you later."

Bud watched as Hawk continued on down the road, leaving a strangeness in his wake which was emphasized by an odd purple light coming from the setting sun, a light that seemed to accentuate the figure receding in the distance, giving it an odd aura.

He sat up straight, his neck stiff from leaning against the FJ seat. He noted that the dogs were still sleeping.

It had to have been a dream. If Hawk had been real, they would've been barking when he walked up.

There were no strange clouds over the Swell, though he could still make out a dark band to the west as if a storm was coming in. The sun hadn't set, and the light was perfectly normal. There was no one walking down the road.

It was another of his strange dreams where his subconscious got tired of him fumbling around and tried to make things clear, though this time, Bud was even more confused.

He'd go home, have a nice dinner, then sleep on it. Maybe things would become clearer in the morning.

With that, he started the FJ and headed back to the bungalow, now thinking only of a nice meatloaf and mashed potatoes dinner, hopefully with some of Wilma Jean's delicious apple pie for dessert— maybe even with a dollop of vanilla-bean ice cream on top.

27

Bud was in his office, thinking about something he'd just read on the Internet, something about the perfect crime.

He was having trouble shaking his dream of the previous afternoon and was looking for something to divert his attention, even though he'd just gotten off the phone with Rachael's daughter, who had confirmed his suspicions by saying she'd gotten the flowers for the memorial service from some guy who called himself the Green River Gopher. She'd paid him well, happy with how fresh everything was.

As if on cue, Molly called.

"Yell-ow," Bud answered.

"Bud, I have a problem out here. I need you to come check it out. Kale won't get involved, saying it's not his deal. I think he's secretly supportive of the whole thing."

"What whole thing?" Bud asked.

"Well, I think Joey's living in the workroom off the garage with Scratch. Every time I feed Scratch, he wants extra to take home for later. I mean, a *lot* extra. And I've caught a glimpse of someone every so often, and it's not Scratch."

"Are you still having things go missing?"

"Thankfully, no."

Bud knew he might have to eventually arrest Joey, but so far, all he had against him was circumstantial evidence, as no one had actually seen him steal anything. There was a good chance, however, that Rachael's daughter would be willing to make a statement against him.

He said, "I thought Joey was helping you out around there."

"Well, he is, but he wasn't around all that much. Now when I need something that Scratch can't do, hard work like digging up weeds, Joey just seems to magically appear after I mention it to Scratch. And his bicycle has been parked behind the rose bushes for several days."

"Are you paying him?"

"Not much. He says he doesn't even want to be paid."

Wondering if Joey might not be feeling a bit guilty, Bud said, "So, you're getting twice the work you were before, and the only difference is you now have to provide some extra food and a little pay. That doesn't sound like a problem to me, Molly, it sounds more like a benefit."

Molly paused as if thinking, then said, "Well, I guess it's all in how you frame it. But he didn't even ask to stay. Do you mind him staying here?"

"Well, Molly, it's more your call than mine, since you manage the place. Whatever you decide is OK by me."

"Maybe I'll just run with it and put Joey to work—I mean, real work, like helping me clean and do laundry. I'll make him sorry he ever showed up in the first place."

"You could build a small empire out there, Molly, even take some time off. You deserve it," Bud said.

"It's going to run the food bill up some, Bud. Are you sure Wilma Jean wouldn't mind?" Molly asked with concern.

Bud replied, "Run it by her if you want, but I know she'll think it's a fine idea if you're comfortable with having them there. With all these artists around, we know you're being overworked. I'd say go for it. It solves your problems and their's, too, it seems. And it sounds like Kale's OK with it."

"Oh, you know him. He's OK with about anything, as long as it doesn't affect his farming. But Bud, there's something else..."

"Go ahead."

"Well, you know that weird toy thing you left here, that doughnut thing?"

"The Gogh-Nut? I forgot all about it, to be honest. I need to get it back. I've been pretty scattered lately."

"Join the club," Molly replied. "But it's gone. It was on the side table in the living room, and as I was cleaning, that couple from Tahoe, Kate and Charles, saw it. I swear, that woman should audition for Hollywood. She'd get an Oscar with her first performance."

Bud asked with concern, "What happened?"

"He showed it to her, and she about had a heart attack. She grabbed it and asked where it came from, then started going on and on about how someone had found it and they needed to go back out somewhere to see if it was OK. I have no idea what *it* referred to, but she was really upset, as usual, although maybe even more so this time."

"Maybe *it* was the Great Attractor," Bud replied, then added, "No, that's not what it was, as it's not capitalized."

"What in the world are you talking about?"

"Never mind. I got carried away. Thanks for the information."

"Do you have any idea what they were talking about? What's a Gogh-Nut, anyway?"

"I think it's a kids' toy. I'll check into it. I think they may have lost it and are wondering who found it."

"She's definitely lost it," Millie said. "I can't wait until they leave."

They hung up, and Bud returned his attention to what he'd been reading on the Internet about the perfect crime, before Molly had called.

He'd been looking at a site about the Zone of Death, which Doc had mentioned in passing when they were out in Black Dragon talking to Scratch about the Zone of Avoidance. Doc had said it was an area in Yellowstone where one couldn't be prosecuted for crimes, and this intrigued Bud. Looking into it, Bud found that it was a

50 square mile area of Yellowstone National Park in Idaho where one could actually commit the perfect crime—that is, do whatever they wanted and avoid prosecution for any major crime, including murder.

Bud wasn't sure he understood it, but the website he'd pulled up read:

> *Since the federal government has exclusive jurisdiction over Yellowstone, crimes committed in the park can't be prosecuted under any states' laws. In addition, the Sixth Amendment to the U.S. Constitution says that juries in federal criminal cases must be made up of citizens who are from both the district and state where the crime was committed. Since the Idaho portion of the park is uninhabited, a jury of residents of both the state and district could not be impaneled. Thus, a defendant facing any felony or misdemeanor charge, being unable to receive a constitutional trial, could not be legally punished regardless of guilt or innocence.*

Bud leaned back in his chair, absent-mindedly running his thumbs up and down his suspenders, wondering if anyone had ever committed a crime there and gotten away with it, though he wasn't sure how anyone would ever know. He continued reading:

> *The constitutional loophole in this area was discovered by Michigan State University law professor Brian C. Kalt while he was planning to write an essay about technicalities of the Sixth Amendment, which entitles criminal defendants to a fair and quick trial. Kalt wondered about a hypothetical place where there were not enough eligible citizens to form a jury and theorized that there could be no trial and therefore no punishment for major crimes in that area. He later realized that there was such a place: the Idaho section of Yellowstone National Park. Horrified by his realization, Kalt shifted his focus to writing an essay called "The Perfect Crime" about the area to persuade the government to fix the loophole. He suggested to lawmakers in Wyoming that the Zone of Death be included as part of the federal district court for the District of Idaho instead of the*

Wyoming district, which would partially fix the issue. However, Congress ignored Kalt's suggestion.

Others have tried to increase governmental awareness with no success. No known felonies have been committed in the Zone of Death since Kalt's discovery.

Completely sidetracked, his dream forgotten, he now suddenly remembered what Molly had said about Kate telling Charles they needed to go back out somewhere to see if something was OK.

Bud knew exactly what that something was—it had to be the grave. He dialed Doc to see if he wanted to go for another ride-along, hoping he and Millie were through playing golf, for he had no desire to go back out to Black Dragon Canyon alone.

Doc said he'd be right there, and he was going to get Howie to come along too. To Bud's relief, they were both soon at Bud's office, the three of them heading on their way back out to the canyon.

28

The trio rode in Doc's black Land Rover, Bud in the back seat with Howie in the front, all munching on the hotdogs and chips Howie had brought.

As they got on the freeway, Doc said to Howie, "Did you know there's a lynch mob looking for you?"

Howie stopped chewing for a moment, then asked, "You're kidding, right?"

Doc grinned. "Millie told me. She said everyone in town's pretty worried about you trying to bring a dairy here. It probably wouldn't be so great for fresh air and all that."

Howie countered, "I already figured that out. I'm going for a chicken farm instead. That way I'll have fresh eggs for my drive-in."

Now it was Doc's turn to say, "You're kidding, right?"

"Are they bad, too?" Howie asked.

"I can tell you grew up in a non-agricultural area," Doc said.

"Sunnyside," Howie replied. "Coal mining. Some people had backyard chickens, though."

"Not the same," Doc said.

Bud sat silently in the back, only half-listening, thinking again about the dream he'd had of the Invisible Man, AKA Hawk. It seemed cryptic and surreal, and yet, he knew everything in it had to be logical, if he could only figure out how. His subconscious might have a warped sense of humor, he thought, but it never led him astray.

He pulled his harmonica from his pocket and began playing *Ghost Riders in the Sky*, thinking.

A number of things had stood out, one being Hawk asking Bud if he could take him back to a previous life, his life before everything got so confusing. Had Hawk somehow reinvented himself into a new life and was now regretting it? Had he maybe changed professions or gotten divorced or even run away from something?

And what about his comment that he wasn't who Bud thought he was, and that they'd never met before. He'd also said none of the artists at the memorial had known Ted. Then why were they there? Hawk had said he'd gone to see if it was his own service, then mentioned Tom Sawyer, as if the service was for someone living, not dead. But Ted was definitely dead.

Howie was now saying something about how it looked like it was going to rain, and Doc was talking about not getting stuck if it did and how hard it was to talk with Bud playing his harmonica, but Bud was now thinking about how Doc had said that the body in the painting might actually be sleeping and not dead.

Interrupting Doc and Howie, Bud asked, "Doc, what did you mean when you said the body might not be dead?"

"What body are you talking about?" Doc asked. "I actually haven't seen any bodies. That was your and Howie's deal."

"No, the body in the painting. Remember when I said they should've painted little x's over its eyes to show it was dead and not sleeping?"

"Bud, there's an old saying that goes you can't wake someone up when they're pretending to be asleep," Doc replied, now turning off the freeway to the wire gate leading into Black Dragon.

"I don't get it," Howie said. "What are you guys talking about?"

"Bingo!" Bud replied, feeling a rushing sense of relief. "If it had been a snake, it would've bit me."

He got out to open the gate, then waited as Doc drove on through, closing it again.

Back in the vehicle, Bud continued. "I think I might have figured out part of what's going on, but I'm not sure. What would you guys say if I told you we had two different guys mixed up?"

"You mean like Ted wasn't really Ted but was someone else?" Howie asked. "But we know it was Ted Henderson. I mean, we even had a memorial service for him and all that—and a coroner's report."

"If there were two different guys, it would explain a lot of things, Howie," Bud replied. "For example, Kate and Charles said they found the body in Double Arch Canyon, but we found it in Black Dragon. What if there were actually two bodies and we only found one of them, one they weren't even aware of?"

"Then what happened to the first body?" Howie asked.

Bud replied, "I walked both canyons looking and found nothing. But maybe it wasn't really a dead body, but a live body. Scratch said he saw someone push someone else off a large rock. What if it didn't kill him, yet whoever pushed him thought it did? Maybe it just knocked him out and he recovered and walked out of the canyon. Stranger things have happened. And Doc, you were already suspecting this, weren't you? Why didn't you tell me what you were thinking?"

Doc replied, "I hinted it at, Bud, but I didn't want to bias your investigation. What if I was wrong?"

"You know, Doc," Bud replied. "I need to talk to Molly, but I have a feeling we're talking about two guys named Ted. One was Ted Henderson, but the other was the Ted at the B&B who got in the fight with Charles."

"If we do have two different Teds," Howie replied. "We need to call them Ted #1 and Ted #2 to keep everything straight. But one of them is still missing."

"Maybe we now have two murders to solve," Doc said, pulling up and parking next to a car near the petroglyphs.

"Or maybe one of the Teds isn't really missing at all, but in disguise," Bud said, thinking about Hawk.

"But what would be the reason behind a disguise?" Doc asked.

Now recalling what Hawk had said about how Bud should consider a death certificate, Bud remembered Charles saying he was going to get one. Bud replied, "I'm not sure, but maybe it has to do with an insurance settlement. Maybe Kate and Charles tried to murder Ted for some kind of insurance, as she was his ex, but they botched it and didn't realize it. They have to be totally confused by now, thinking they went to *their* Ted's memorial when it was actually Ted Henderson's. Hawk said it was really simple, that I had the answers."

"When did you talk to Hawk?" Howie asked.

Bud was silent, not wanting to say it had all been a cryptic dream.

"Are you going to arrest them for attempted murder, Sheriff?" Howie asked as Doc parked near the petroglyphs. They all got out near the car, which had California plates.

"I need more evidence, Howie," Bud replied, thinking of what Hawk had said about how he had a witness, if he would just listen to him. "An accusation of murder is a pretty serious thing, and you'd better have some good evidence for it. I dropped the ball on doing a more in-depth interview with Scratch, as he said he saw everything. But I think I have an even better witness—Ted himself—who was there."

"We definitely need to start calling them Ted #1 and Ted #2," Howie said. "I'm losing track."

"I know the feeling," Bud replied. "But when we went into Black Dragon, remember we saw a vehicle with Nevada plates out by the draw going into Double Arch? That was Ted's vehicle, Ted #1, the one Kate and Charles reported as being dead. He was still in there when we came in, but he left before we came out. If you recall, the car was gone when we came back out with Ted #2's body. And I saw Ted #1 driving that same car at the B&B, posing as Hawk. That, along with Doc's comment and my dream, led me to maybe figuring things out."

"What dream?" Doc asked.

"I'll tell you about it later," Bud replied. "I think I may owe Rachael an apology for making her think her husband had been staying at the B&B, as that had to be Ted #1, not her Ted. But for now, from the looks of the California plates on this car, we need to go see what's going on at that grave we dug up."

"If you're thinking of Kate and Charles, wouldn't they have Nevada plates?" Doc asked. "I thought they were all from Tahoe."

"Lake Tahoe straddles Nevada and California," Bud replied. "There are towns on both sides, but people tend to refer to everything as just Tahoe. So one could have plates from either state, depending on exactly where you lived."

Howie asked, "But why would they have buried some ashes and toys in a grave?"

"Not to mention a priceless Van Gogh painting," Bud added.

"A Van Gogh? Is that what was in that package?" Doc asked.

Bud replied, "I'm no art expert, Doc, but I would swear it's the real deal."

"Bury an authentic Van Gogh out here in Black Dragon? Who would do that? It might risk ruining it." Howie said.

"Agreed," Bud agreed. "And it's supposed to be in some Van Gogh museum, so I suspect it's stolen, which would explain trying to hide it."

Now Doc said with concern, "Fellows, it's starting to sprinkle. We need to hoof it to the grave and then get out of here. We won't have any trouble here in the canyon, as it's all sand, but that stretch from the wash to the freeway is pure mud when it's wet."

"Let's go," Bud said, wondering what the next few minutes would bring, both in terms of the rain and, thinking of Kate, in terms of drama.

29

As they walked down the canyon, Bud began thinking about something he'd always wondered as a kid—why his Grandpa O'Connor's dress pants had buttons sewn into the waist. He'd never figured it out until now, and it seemed like an odd thing to come to him just then, but he'd just made the connection—metal clasps on the ends of suspenders hadn't yet been invented, and one buttoned them to their pants.

"Slow down, guys," Bud said. "I just figured something important out."

Doc and Howie stopped, waiting for Bud to catch up, looking at him questioningly. When he told them, Howie started laughing.

"I think maybe you need a break, Sheriff," he said.

"Did you know that Mark Twain had one of the first patents for suspenders?" Doc added. "But is there some connection here we're missing?"

"I don't know," Bud replied. "It just popped into my brain, but maybe there is a connection."

"It has to be symbolic or something, if there is," Howie replied. "Something not very obvious. I mean, we're on the trail of possible criminals and a suspicious grave, and you're thinking about suspenders?"

"I think wearing suspenders tells the world you're a diligent sleuth," Bud said. "Nothing can stop you from getting the job done because you don't have to worry about being caught with your pants down."

"I don't know about that, but we need to get out of here soon," Doc said. "It's starting to sprinkle."

They were soon standing over the grave, which had obviously been dug up, with no effort to refill it.

"It looks like they must've just left," Doc said quietly. "They have to be nearby."

"How can you tell?" Howie asked.

Doc replied, "You can still smell the dirt, and it doesn't smell like that unless it's been freshly turned. I do a lot of gardening and notice things like that."

They poked around for awhile, but seeing nothing new decided to head back to the vehicle, as a light drizzle was starting.

"Their car's still here," Bud noted as they got into Doc's vehicle out of the rain. "But where are they?"

"I have a feeling they're hiding from us," Howie said. "They know what we both look like after meeting us in your office, Bud, and they may have heard us coming, as we weren't trying to be quiet. I would guess they don't want to meet up with the sheriff, especially after finding out their grave's been discovered."

"If they don't get out soon, they won't be getting out at all," Doc said. "The weather report this morning said we're in for a couple of days of rain."

"Maybe they'll come out if we start yelling," Bud said, then proceeded to call out their names, which echoed down the canyon. They waited for awhile, then they all yelled together, but there was no response, the rain now getting heavier by the minute.

"We need to go," Doc said. "No point is us getting stuck. Having a four-wheel drive does no good in gumbo."

Everyone now in Doc's Land Rover, they high-tailed it out of the canyon, leaving the car with the California plates behind. Once near the wash that drained from Double Arch Canyon, they had a few exciting moments when the Rover slid and they thought they were going to get stuck, but Doc, an experienced driver, gunned his way out, and they were soon back at the gate by the freeway.

"I have a really bad feeling about this," Bud said as he returned from opening and closing the gate. "It doesn't seem right to leave them in there. Let's sit here for awhile and see if they don't come out soon."

Doc pulled over and turned off the engine, the rain now pelting the vehicle's roof, sounding like it would soon turn to hail.

"They're coming!" Howie said excitedly, pointing to a set of head-lights through the rain.

Bud jumped out and met them at the gate, opening it. As they slid through, their car coated with mud where the tires had flung it up, he waved for them to stop. He could clearly see it was Kate and Charles, but they gunned the car up onto the blacktop and off towards Green River.

"Follow that car," Bud told Doc as he got back in after closing the gate. "I don't have any way of telling, but I think they're speeding."

Doc laughed, obviously relieved. "I doubt if I can catch up with them, Sheriff. And how do I pull them over with no siren or lights?"

"I hope we don't have any gunplay," Howie said, half-joking. "At least we know where they live."

The closer they got to town, the lighter the rain got, until it completely stopped. Bud turned to look behind them, and the Swell was shrouded in black clouds which he knew would continue to move in, though slowly.

It would be a good time to get some office work done, but for now, he wanted to go on out to the Melon View B&B and see if Kate and Charles were there. Besides, he had something he wanted to ask Molly.

"Let's go back to my office, Doc. I want to show you guys that painting, and I need to get my vehicle. I want to go out to the B&B."

They were soon studying the Van Gogh, which Bud had again carefully unwrapped and leaned against the wall.

"Would you look at that!" Doc exclaimed in awe. "No wonder the guy's famous. That's truly something else."

"I've never been a Van Gogh fan," Howie said. "But this is incredible. And Sheriff, I'm no art critic, but it does look authentic. I see what you mean by seeing the painter's brush swirls and everything."

"That style of painting is called impasto," Doc said. The paint is put on so thick you can see the brush strokes. Some artists even mix the colors right on the canvas. It's used for texture, to give the painting a 3D effect."

"Is that something Van Gogh did a lot?" Bud asked.

"Yes, in his painting *Starry Night* he wanted to make the stars appear as bright as possible, so he used an extremely thick consistency with bold brush-strokes."

"I didn't know you were an art critic, Doc," Howie said.

"I'm not much of one," he replied. "But I tried my hand at oils once many years ago when I was with my first wife. It was more of a way to tune her out than a true interest. I quickly realized I was cut out to be a doctor, not an artist, which I was grateful for, as I like to eat."

"The old starving artist thing, eh?" Bud asked. "But if you could paint like Van Gogh, you'd be rich."

"Actually, Sheriff, he died in poverty," Howie said. "But what are you going to do with this? Any idea where it came from? Did they steal it?"

"I have no idea, Howie," Bud replied. "But for now, I'm going to wrap it back up and put it in the safe. I did a little research on it, and it's supposed to be owned by some Van Gogh museum, so when I get time, I'm going to call them and see what's going on. But right now, I'm going out to the B&B and see if they went back there, and there's something I need to talk to Molly about."

"I should go make some barbecue sauce," Howie said.

"I take it you're hiding out from that lynch mob?" Doc grinned.

"I'll come and serve as a body guard if you'll show me how to make your secret sauce. Millie says it's the best she's ever had."

Doc and Howie walked across the street to Mayor Howie's Drive-In, leaving Bud to ponder the latest in his sleuthing attempts, which didn't seem like they were going much of anywhere lately.

Maybe Molly could shed some light on things, he thought, locking the office and getting into his sheriff's Land Cruiser.

30

"Molly, can I look through your sign-in sheet for guests?" Bud asked as Molly set out a plate of homemade fudge for the B&B guests.

"It's over on that table, Bud. Help yourself."

Flipping back a few pages, he finally found where Hawk had signed in: *Hawk Papillon, Sego, Utah, Social Entrepreneur.* Looking at the writing, Bud felt it was contrived, as it seemed shaky and scribbled. Nevertheless, he took out the Perfect Crime letter, holding it next to the signature and trying to compare the two.

So far, nothing matched at all, which made sense, seeing how little he had to go on with just a signature. He felt defeated, but continued studying both, until he thought he saw one small similarity—the capital *S* in *Sego* had a small curl at the top, and so did the *S* in the word *Starry*. Looking closer, he decided they could have been made by the same person, though he knew it wasn't much to go on.

If he was right, then the Perfect Crime letter had been written by Hawk, though he knew it wasn't enough to be definitive. And if his earlier assumptions were correct, Hawk was Ted #1, the same man who had gotten in a fight with Charles earlier and injured his hand.

He thought back—hadn't Hawk had a bandage on his hand that

time he'd come into the Melon Rind Cafe? And he'd been wearing gloves the rest of the time, as if to hide it.

Molly had gone into the kitchen and was now back out, handing Bud a cup of coffee.

"Did you find what you were looking for?" She asked.

"I'm not sure, but maybe," Bud replied, taking a sip from the hot cup. "This is delicious."

"It's some Wilma Jean brought out. She's been ordering it in from some place in Salt Lake called Wicked Brew. Everyone loves it."

"Molly," Bud said. "I've been thinking. You know when Ted left you said he took a set of towels, but could it be possible that someone else stole them, maybe the same someone who's been stealing other things?"

"Possibly, but it's *Tad*, Bud."

"Right," Bud frowned, then added, "Wait, did you say Tad? Isn't his name Ted?"

"He registered as Tad Hall, from Lake Tahoe, Nevada."

"Not Ted?"

"Tad from Tahoe."

"Maybe you misread his name," Bud said.

"I try to learn all my guests' names, Bud. And that's what everyone was calling him—Tad. But what's going on?"

"Apparently a case of mistaken identity, Molly, that's all. Some poor sleuthing on my part."

"Well, Ted and Tad do sound a lot alike."

"Molly, can I use your computer for a minute?"

"Of course. Go on in the office." She pointed him to a small room off the kitchen, where he was soon booted up doing a search.

The name Tad is a boy's name. Full name options include Thaddeus and Thomas, which was the given name of Abe's son Tad Lincoln. Ted, however, is a boy's name of Greek origin. Typically this is a short form of Theodore or even Edward in some cases.

Bud sighed. How could something so simple become so convoluted, causing so much confusion? If he'd only paid attention, he was sure Molly at some point had called him Tad, not Ted, and yet he'd made the erroneous assumption that there was only one character in the play, and his name was Ted Henderson.

Molly was now back in the kitchen, and Bud called out, "Molly, can you come in here for a minute?"

He said, "I have a confession to make. I screwed up royally thinking Tad was Ted. I'm responsible for Ted Henderson's wife Rachael thinking he was staying out here, when it was Tad all the time, no connection whatsoever."

Surprised, Molly said, "It's OK, Bud. We all make mistakes."

"But this one was a doozy, Molly. I have a number of people thinking things that aren't true."

"Like who, besides Rachael? I'm sure once you tell her all this, she'll be fine. I just hope she doesn't come out here again. It's going to be awhile before I stop feeling resentful about her assuming there was something going on between me and her husband."

"I'm sure she'll feel bad, but not as bad as I feel."

"It's all over and done with, Bud. Don't worry about it. I'm more worried about the fact that Kate and Charles told me they're leaving several days early, as in today. They want a refund, but Bud, I'm not sure if I can fill their room now, as things are slowing down."

"They're leaving today?"

"They're up in their room packing right now. Oh, and I forgot to tell you. Kate tried to destroy the canvas in the living room. She had a fit and got some scissors and was going to cut it up, but Charles stopped her. A lot of the artists have added to it and it's getting to be really nice. I'm glad they're leaving, though we'll probably lose some money, unless I refuse to refund their room."

"Why would she want to destroy the painting?"

"Someone painted a really ugly big black wolf-like dog on it, and she said it was getting too personal. Charles apologized for her, but he said someone here was taunting her. I have no idea what he was talking about."

"Molly, is it tea-time yet?"

"Not for another hour, but I can bring you a scone if you want."

"No, listen, go tell Charles and Kate that you're going to have tea early on their behalf since they're leaving and you really want them to stay for it, one last chance to see them. And tell them you're waiting for some cash to show up before you can refund their room—whatever it takes to detain them for awhile. I have something I need to work on before they can leave, and I need your help."

"OK, I'll do what I can."

"Do you know where Scratch is?"

"He and Joey are out weeding. I didn't have anything for them to do, so Kale is putting them to work."

"OK, thanks," Bud said as Molly headed upstairs. He needed to find Scratch, and quickly, before Charles and Kate left, for he suspected the couple had tried to murder Tad, and it all had something to do with the mysterious and possibly stolen Van Gogh.

But he also knew you couldn't detain a suspect on suspicions. Heading for the field to find Scratch, he felt he was quickly losing confidence in his sleuthing abilities.

Maybe it was time to concede defeat and admit that perhaps the perfect crime had indeed been committed, and like the letter had said, he would never know what it was or who it involved.

31

Bud sat under a big cottonwood tree on the farm, cottonwood seeds flying all around him and landing in his hair, turning it white. The sweet smell of Russian olive blooms drifted through the air, and he thought it would be a perfect day except for everything that was going on.

Across from him sat Scratch and Joey, the latter who he'd never met until just then. Joey had light blonde hair and was much younger than Bud had thought, or maybe he just looked young for his age, as Molly had said he was in high school, but to Bud he looked like maybe middle school.

Even though sitting under the big cottonwoods along the farm's irrigation ditches was one of his favorite things to do, Bud felt a sense of urgency, for he knew Molly wouldn't be able to detain the couple for long, and he wanted to talk to them before they left, maybe even arrest them.

But he needed evidence of a crime before he could arrest anyone, and so far, he wasn't having much luck. Scratch had seen them in Double Arch with someone Bud knew had to be Tad, and upon further questioning had told Bud he'd seen people pushing each other around, but his eyewitness account of who had actually pushed who off the rock was lacking in a few details—namely *exactly* who had pushed who.

He at first said it was the woman who had pushed the man, but he then admitted they were all too far away for him to be certain, and then he'd told Bud he'd been drinking a lot of tea that day with Ted Henderson, who'd been showing him some photography tricks, and things had gotten a bit sketchy on the eye-witness front.

Thinking back about the alkaloids in Ted's body, Bud had wanted to ask what kind of tea, but decided he'd save that for another day, as he was in a hurry. But Scratch's account did jibe with what Bud knew about Ted having been in Double Arch canyon the same time Kate and Charles were there, and he knew Tad had been there, too. It was all too confusing.

He made a mental note to talk to Scratch later and see if he could figure out what had happened to Ted, but at the moment he was too distracted by the thought that Charles and Kate were leaving.

He could now feel a sense of futility rising in his chest, and he flashed back to all the times he'd sat under these same cottonwoods playing ball with the dogs, not a care in the world. He wished it was like that now, and he had an urge to take out his harmonica, like he'd done so many times before, and play a tune or two.

But he was still hopeful that Scratch and Joey would provide him with some kind of helpful information. Joey seemed to be a nice kid, even if he was a suspected thief, and Bud wondered if he would end up living a life of crime.

Since he couldn't fiddle with his harmonica, he began rubbing his thumbs up and down his suspenders, a substitute, though a poor one, in his opinion.

"My grandpa wears braces, just like you," Joey was saying. "He sometimes calls them galluses. He says belts are bad, as they cut the body in half, and galluses make a heavy man look distinguished. Those look real nice on you, Sheriff—not to imply you're heavy or anything."

Bud was surprised, as he'd asked Joey a few questions earlier, and he'd seemed reticent and unwilling to talk. Obviously, the suspenders were reminding him of his grandfather, who he seemed fond of.

"Where does your grandpa live, Joey?" Bud asked.

"He's on the farm in Nebraska. I'm thinking I should go back there. My parents just moved there. I wanted to stay and finish high school here, and it's over now."

"Just how old are you?" Bud asked.

"Seventeen."

"Too young for prison," Bud said more to himself, then added, "But not too young for reform school—that's what they called it when I was a kid. I almost got sent there myself."

"Reform school?" Joey asked with alarm.

"Oh, I don't mean you personally, just whoever's been stealing things around here and in town."

Bud was now completely sidetracked. He knew he wasn't going to get any information about Kate and Charles from Joey, so he was going with this opportunity to question him about all the petty thefts going on.

"What kind of missing things?" Joey asked.

"Well, for one, steaks," Bud replied.

"I did it, and I'm not proud of it," Joey said quietly.

Surprised, Bud added, "And flowers."

"I did it, and I'm not proud of it," Joey said again.

"And food," Bud added. "Also a set of towels."

"I did it, and I'm not proud of it."

Bud wanted to laugh both at how easy it was to get Joey to confess and also at how he kept repeating himself, but he managed to look stern.

"Do you think that saying that over and over will convince me that what you did is OK because you're not proud of it?"

Joey replied, "No, not really. But I'm also not proud of saying that I'm not proud to try to convince you. I want to make restitution and then leave and go home. If Scratch here hadn't helped me out, and Molly, too, I'd probably be in jail by now. But I've learned there are right ways to do things and wrong ways, and I'm not proud of how long it took me to learn the difference."

Bud was astounded. Joey and Scratch had obviously been talking about things, for Joey certainly hadn't come to this conclusion by himself.

"One more question, Joey," Bud said. "Were people asking you to get things for them, like flowers, and they paid you, then you stole whatever they'd ordered and pocketed the money instead of paying for the stuff? Who asked you to get them steaks?"

"I dunno, just one of the people staying there. He was one of the artists and said he wanted to treat everyone for his birthday."

Bud stood. "Joey, I'm proud of you for being so honest. I'll come back later and we can talk about all this some more, but right now I need to figure out how to keep some folks from running off without paying." He was reluctant to tell them the real reason he needed to go back to the B&B.

Joey also stood, saying, "Sheriff, while you were asking Scratch here about those people, I was afraid to tell you what I know, because I wasn't supposed to be in the B&B. I'd gone inside looking for Molly, even though she said I wasn't allowed to go in without her being there."

He continued. "I heard that couple talking and saying they were going to bury some painting with Black Dragon."

"Don't you mean *in* Black Dragon?" Bud asked.

"No they definitely said *with* Black Dragon. She kept crying, and he said she needed to pull herself together, and she said, 'I can't help but feel bad, I've had him since he was a baby. I bottle fed him, he was my best friend and companion, and I can't help but cry.' Well, the guy, he sounded like he felt really bad, and he told her that he didn't realize Dragon meant so much to her, though he had suspected as much, but he wasn't there when it all started because she was married to this other guy Tad at the time. I don't know what they were talking about, but there you have it."

Bud now had the sinking feeling that he'd botched everything again. Black Dragon? It had to be the name of a dog, or else the couple were exceptionally eccentric at naming their kids. If it were a dog, it would account for the size of the grave, the stuffed animals and the small blanket, as well as all the chew marks on the Gogh-Nut. And the words *Inedible Joy* on the Gogh-Nut meant it was like a dog's Kong toy, something they couldn't destroy and swallow.

But even if the grave belonged to a dog, there was still the matter of the stolen Van Gogh painting, and his prime suspects were getting ready to leave, with him having no way to detain them.

He said goodbye to Scratch and Joey and headed back to the Melon View B&B, wishing he was on his way out to the Big Empty with the dogs and wondering if maybe he shouldn't quit as sheriff and stick to melon farming.

He'd done it before, and maybe it was time to accept that he was losing his edge.

32

Bud was back in Molly's office, standing in front of the community painting, studying what appeared to be a snarling dire wolf. It was painted where the dead body had been, and even though Bud had thought it was an improvement, it still didn't fit the rest of the painting, which had become a beautiful canyon scene with creamy-white Datura and a double arch.

The animal was coal black and, now knowing what to call the style, was painted in impasto, just like the Datura, hawkmoth, and body had been. It was well done, and whoever painted it had talent. It was kind of spooky looking with its glaring red eyes and its lips snarled back to show large yellow menacing teeth—not at all what someone would view as a pet, Bud mused.

Molly had told him she'd talked Charles and Kate into staying the remainder of their reservation by telling them she was going to remove the painting from the B&B. She'd put it in her office where no one could see it and was keeping the door locked.

Bud was perplexed, wondering why anyone would ruin a perfectly nice painting. He was beginning to feel that being confused was becoming his normal state these days.

But hadn't Charles said that whoever was doing it was getting too personal? Was the wolf-dog supposed to depict the dog they'd called Black Dragon? If so, it seemed to Bud that the painter was trying to depict a beloved pet as a ruthless killer, which would upset anyone.

Molly now tapped lightly on the door, then opened it and came in, closing it behind her.

"Have you figured out what's going on, Bud?" She asked.

"I think Kate had a dog and someone is trying to make it look vicious. That's why she got so upset. I think they buried it out in the canyons."

"Well, that would explain why she's been so emotional. If I'd just lost my dog, I'd be upset, too. But that looks more like a wolf than a dog. What kind of dog was it?"

"I don't know, maybe a German Shepherd or something like that. Some kind of big dog. Joey said she called it Black Dragon."

"That's an odd name. It sounds like something a dog breeder would come up with for a sire or show dog. They have all kinds of weird names. Have you ever heard of Baron von Heathertoes? He was a famous dachshund. And there was Horand von Grafrath, who was the first registered German Shepherd. And Lord Snuggles, another dachshund. And then there was Rin Tin Tin." She smiled and added, "And Hoppie and Pierre and Lindie."

Bud laughed, then asked, "Can I use your computer again? I want to do a quick search, then I need to get back to my office. Thanks for convincing them to stay, by the way."

"No problem," Molly replied, leaving and closing the door behind her. Bud was glad she didn't know the real reason he wanted the couple to stay and just thought it was so they didn't have to refund their money.

He quickly looked up a number, then started to dial it, but then realized it was a foreign number. Opening the office door, he called out to Molly, who was nearby in the kitchen.

"How do I dial an international number?"

"Just dial 011 and the number," she replied.

He closed the door, made sure it was locked, then dialed.

A man's voice answered in a language Bud didn't recognize, though he was able to make out the words *Van Gogh Museum*.

Bud said, "Do you speak English?"

The voice replied, "Yes. Jort Slingerland speaking. How may I help you?"

"Mr. Slingerland, my name is Bud Shumway, and I'm in the United States. You're in the Netherlands, right? Amsterdam?"

"That's right."

"I'm calling about a painting that your website says is in your permanent collection there. It's called *Wheatfield under Thunderclouds*. I know this is going to sound odd, but is it still there?"

"Last I looked it was. And yes, it *is* an odd question."

"And what is your position there, if I may ask?"

"I'm Head of Operations. I manage the Security, Visitor Services, Support Services, and ICT departments."

"So you would be one to definitely know if a painting was missing or not."

"I would. But what's this about, Mr. Shumway?"

"I'm wondering what a painting like that would be worth. Do you have any idea?"

"It would be invaluable. It was painted in 1890. Similar ones have sold for over 50 million euros. That's almost 47 million in U.S. dollars. Are you thinking of stealing it?"

Bud laughed nervously. "No, no, but I thought maybe I'd found the original. It looks like it—it even has the impasto and all."

"Are you an art collector, Mr. Shumway?"

"No, I'm a sheriff. I thought I had a stolen painting."

"Well, you may have, but it's not the original. I can assure you it's safe and sound here in the museum. You should come visit us sometime. We have many original Van Goghs. We have had thefts, but the paintings have always been recovered."

Bud, sensing the man was about to hang up on him, asked, "If a painting had the same kind of 3D texture as the original, what would one think? Help me out here, as I don't know anything about art—except that I really love Van Gogh."

He hoped the part about Van Gogh would soften the guy up.

"Well, it's quite possible that you have a Fujifilm replica. That particular painting is one of the nine paintings we've released in that mode. The collection features a limited print run of 260 reproductions of each of the featured masterworks."

"What does that mean?" Bud asked.

"The museum partnered with Fujifilm Belgium a number of years ago to create three-dimensional replicas of Van Gogh's most famous pieces. It's accomplished through a process called Reliefography. They combine a 3D scan of a given work with a high-quality print, and the result is nearly indistinguishable from the original. It's done on a 3D printer. The reproductions are of such high quality that it is almost impossible to distinguish them from the originals with the naked eye. Van Gogh often used thick applications of paint on his canvas, making his works perfectly suited for 3D reproduction."

"No kidding!" Bud replied. "And what would one of these be worth?"

"The museum sells that particular Relievo, which is what they're called, for nearly $40,000 euros. We have a number of others, if you're interested. These are very high-end reproductions, and you simply can't get closer to the original. All come with a certificate of authenticity."

"I'll have to think about it," Bud replied. "My wife might like one for her birthday, but she'll have to take down her Monet to make room for it. But thanks for the information. You've been very helpful."

"You're quite welcome," the man said, then just before hanging up added, "Keep our number."

"I'll keep it on my speed dial," Bud said, grinning, relieved to know the painting wasn't an original Van Gogh. But he still didn't understand why someone would spend that kind of money on a reproduction and then bury it in a dog's grave. It didn't make sense.

It then occurred to him that he needed to get the dog's ashes and toys back to Kate and let her know her dog was OK—well, as OK as a dead dog could be. And he then needed to question her and Charles about the Van Gogh and why they'd buried it. He was sure the BLM had some kind of rules about burying things on public land.

It was just another strange task that went with this whole perfect crime fiasco, he thought, and even though he figured he now had a good idea who'd written the perfect crime letter, he was no closer to knowing why, nor to knowing what had happened to the photographer Ted Henderson.

33

Bud and Doc sat in the back booth of the Melon Rind Cafe, drinking coffee and waiting for Howie to show up so they could go to the airport, as it was the last day of the RC show.

Bud asked, "Doc, why would someone paint things that they knew would upset someone else?"

"You mean that painting out at the B&B?" Doc asked. "I was trying to keep an eye on it, but it seems to have disappeared."

"Molly put it in her office and shut it all down after someone painted a wolf-like dog on it. It seems that Kate is being harassed, and it has to be someone staying there. But why would someone use that medium? It seems like there would be lots more effective ways to get to someone."

"What all's been painted? Every time I saw it, it looked pretty normal to me," Doc asked. "Except that time there was a body."

"That's because they always paint over the previous thing. It started with a Datura and hawkmoth, then the hawkmoth was painted over by a dead hawkmoth, then it was that body—that was right after you arrived—then it was the dog painted over the body."

"And it's always the same artist?"

Bud replied, "It appears to be. Someone who uses the impasta technique, like Van Gogh."

"That Charles fellow seems to be a Van Gogh fan, from the looks of his t-shirts," Doc said. "And it's *impasto*, not impasta, not like something you'd eat."

"Sounds good," Bud replied. "And if that was their dog in the grave in Black Dragon, they even got it Van Gogh toys, like the Gogh-Nut."

"And the letter you got had a reference to Van Gogh and was signed Vinnie. It has to all be related, Bud, and there has to be a logical explanation."

"And I think it all revolves around Kate. Someone's carrying a big grudge and trying to get back at her for something. And if that painting in the grave is stolen, that may be why."

"So, you're thinking that she stole the Van Gogh painting, and whoever she stole it from is maybe trying to get back at her through emotional harassment? But who would it be? You said it has to be someone staying at the B&B."

Bud replied, "It has to be an artist, someone who's good at painting, for the style was really well done. And they have to be staying there."

"Could they come in the middle of the night and do it?" Doc asked.

"Molly locks everything up after 10 p.m."

"Maybe someone with a key?"

"Maybe, but it makes more sense for it to be someone staying there, then they could just slip down after everyone's in bed and do the deed. If someone caught them, they could just say they couldn't sleep and were trying their hand at adding to the painting."

"Makes sense. But who could it be?"

Bud replied, "I don't know. There are a number of people staying there, and they're all artists except that strange fellow Hawk."

"What is it with that guy, anyway?" Doc asked. "He never talks to anyone and is covered from head to toe."

"Molly said he told her he has a skin condition. Howie calls him the Invisible Man. But Doc, I had a strange dream about him, and he said some really odd things to me."

"Oh, boy, another of those dreams," Doc replied.

"They can be pretty cryptic, Doc, but they usually help me figure things out."

"Yes, the subconscious mind loves being cryptic and working in symbols. What did he say in the dream?"

"I wrote it all down afterwards." Bud pulled a small piece of paper from his pocket, then studied it.

"Well, for one thing, he said he wanted to go back to his previous life when things weren't so complicated. That was the first thing he said, basically."

"Probably before he became the Invisible Man," Doc said.

"But who was he before that?"

Doc asked, "Is he actually invisible? Maybe he was someone who was *very* visible, like a celebrity or something."

"Maybe a famous artist," Bud replied. "Then he said that Kate and Charles were basically thieves and liars. He said his ex-wife wanted revenge since she didn't get everything in the divorce. Then he said *I*, of all people, should know what she stole."

"Cryptic."

Bud continued. "He also said he went to Ted's memorial to see if it was his own service, but it wasn't, and I should consider a death certificate."

"Do you have any idea what it all means? It was a dream, after all, not the real Hawk. Maybe your subconscious has things mixed up."

"Very possible," Bud replied. "But he also said things were simple, and I had a witness."

"Who would that be?" Doc asked.

"I thought of Scratch, but he really didn't see things all that well. He actually wasn't much help. He saw people pushing each other around, but couldn't really identify anyone in particular. But Doc, one thing he said was a direct quote from the book by H.G. Wells. He said, 'I'm invisible, and there are lots of wild and wonderful things I now have the impunity to do.'"

"Like maybe paint weird things on canvases?"

Bud was silent for awhile. "I've been wondering if Hawk is the one doing that, and if he's really Tad."

"It's just a thought, Bud. If he's not who he says he is, like he told you, then he's somebody else, isn't he?"

Bud replied, "I have had a hunch that he's involved in all this somehow. He also said in the dream that he liked looking like Groucho Marx because it confuses people. I think he's Tad in disguise."

"Tad seems to have just disappeared, hasn't he?" Doc asked.

"Yes, and no one ever found his body. I think that was his car that Howie and I saw when we first went into the canyon, and it was gone when we came back. And guess who's driving one just like it?"

"The Invisible Man?"

"Bingo," Bud replied.

"But why would he tell you to get a death certificate?"

"I'm not sure he was saying that, Doc. He just said something about a death certificate, and Charles asked me where the body was so he could get a death certificate for the family. I just assumed it was because there were kids or something and they would need to be able to verify everything for his estate. But maybe there was something else going on. Like maybe some life insurance."

Doc said, "It would be my guess that they're going to have trouble getting that certificate, since he's not dead. But here comes Howie. He said there were going to be wingwalkers at the RC air show today."

"Wingwalkers? Who would be tiny enough to be a wingwalker on a remote-controlled airplane?"

"I don't know. He just said their names were Sharon and Danielle."

"They have names? Maybe they're some kind of trained birds. Do they wear little capes?"

"You could probably train pigeons to do something like that," Doc replied.

"Like what?" Howie asked as he came in the door. "You fellas ready to go? I packed us each a sack lunch. Did you know that Charles Lindbergh began his aviation career as a wingwalker?"

They were soon on their way to the airport, Bud distracted, pretty sure now that Hawk and Tad were one and the same. He'd find out soon enough, he figured, as he intended to go back to the B&B as soon as he could.

34

As they headed for the airport, Howie asked, "If you saw your own mom running a stop sign, would you give her a ticket?"

Doc laughed. "Did your mom run a stop sign, Howie?"

Howie, looking troubled, replied, "Not that I know of, but I was reading about this cop over in Colorado, and he gave his own mom a ticket. I mean, I understand pledging to uphold the law and all that, but your own mom?"

"Maybe someone was watching, and he didn't want to be accused of favoritism," Doc replied. "He probably tore up the ticket later. But what's this you were saying about wingwalkers?"

Howie replied, "Eldon was telling me about it. These guys have twin one-third scale biplanes outfitted with wingwalkers. It's like a flying circus! They have little animated models bolted to the wings that you can operate with a control and servos that move the arms and legs. One person operates the plane, and another does the wingwalker."

"Do you suppose the models do it for the money or for the fame and glory?" Doc asked.

"They probably do it for the thrill," Bud replied. "Or maybe because they have no choice."

Howie continued. "They're modeled after the original Stearman biplanes. The pilot sits in the back cockpit because there aren't any controls in the forward cockpit, as a control column would prevent the wingwalkers from climbing onto the upper wing for their act."

"And real people actually did this wingwalking thing?" Doc asked as they arrived at the airport.

"You can still see real wingwalkers at airshows," Howie replied. "They have to soup up the engines on the planes, as the wingwalkers act like giant air brakes since their bodies create a lot of drag."

Parking and walking to the airstrip, they could see two red-and-white radio-controlled biplanes ready to take off, tiny figures standing on top. Several people stood nearby holding controllers.

Doc said, "Must be the wingwalkers Sharon and Danielle. But Howie, you're saying real wingwalkers climb out of the airplane while it's in flight and do gymnastics on the wings to entertain the crowd? Sounds kind of sketchy. I'd hate to see one bite the dust."

"They're cabled to the plane, though Eldon said sometimes they'll release the cable to thrill the crowd. But yeah, it does sound kind of suicidal," Howie replied.

"Remember that 1959 movie *North by Northwest* where Gary Grant is chased by a machine-gun toting crop-duster?" Doc asked. "That was a Stearman biplane."

"That was a bit before my time," Howie replied.

"You didn't have to be around back then to watch it," Doc said. "It's still available."

Just then, a portly man wearing coveralls walked over to them, eyeing Bud's suspenders and saying, "Afternoon, Sheriff."

Then, talking low so only Bud could hear him, he added, "It's a sad day when the sheriff steals from his own constituents."

Bud replied, "Afternoon, George. What sheriff would that be, exactly?"

Looking at Bud knowingly, George replied, "My name is George Wilcox. *GW* are *my* initials."

"I'm pretty sure I knew that already," Bud said, perplexed.

George thumped each of Bud's suspenders with his thumb, saying slowly, "G...W..."

Bud frowned, looking down at the suspenders, then said, "My wife got these at Wiggin's Diggins up in Price. Are you saying they're yours?"

"Sure as eggs is eggs. They went missing, and my wife says she knows nothing about it. I had them custom made with my own initials."

"Well, whoever stole them fenced them at Wiggins Diggins up in Price. Maybe you should keep them locked up, George. Do you have a reward out for them?"

George frowned. "I knew Emma took them to the second-hand shop. She hated those things."

"You can have them if you want."

"Are you serious? I can pay you whatever you paid for them."

"No, that's OK. My wife bought them and they're kind of wearing me out. I don't like the attention, and people keep asking me who *GW* is."

"Well, you're too thin for them anyway. I'll take you up on your offer if you're serious, though Emma's gonna be mad at me. I hate wearing a belt."

Bud unhooked the front of the suspenders, made sure his pants weren't going to fall off, then had Doc unclip the backs.

"Here you go, George. Enjoy them."

George replied, "Thanks, Sheriff. I'm tickled pink—not just to have them back, but because Emma's gonna wonder where in heck they came from. I'll enjoy seeing her squirm. She told me she had no idea what happened to them."

"How do you know they don't belong to someone else with the same initials?" Doc asked.

George held them up, saying, "Very unlikely, but see this little hole here? I accidentally caught them in a fishing hook down at the river. They're the same pair, all right."

George now moved closer to Bud as if wanting to tell him something in private. "Sheriff, I don't know if you've noticed, but everyone's wondering what those two guys are doing around town."

"What two guys?" Bud asked.

Pointing to two men standing by the airstrip, one holding a camera, George replied, "Those two. They've been all over town the last few days, filming anything and everything. Everyplace you go, they're there—the museum, Jay's Tavern, the raft takeout at the state park, the golf course—even Wanda the mail carrier can't figure out what they're up to."

Bud grimaced. "They were in the cafe the other day. If Wanda can't figure it out, it must be something pretty secretive."

"Agreed. She actually asked them and they said they were just tourists."

"How do we know they're not?" Bud asked.

"Tourists don't run around like it's their job to film everything. These guys act like they're making a movie of the area."

"Maybe they are," Howie replied.

"Well, Mayor, you of all people should know what's going on, but I bet you don't, do you?" George asked.

Howie replied, "Maybe I do, maybe I don't."

"If they're up to another of your great economic development ideas, we should run them off."

Bud replied, "Now George, we all know our mayor has the best interests of Green River in mind. He's just trying to make our economy a bit more viable."

"Well, no offense meant, but some of us think his economics ideas are certifiable," George said. "But the wingwalkers are getting started. See you boys later, and thanks for the suspenders, Sheriff."

As George walked off, Howie asked, "What did he mean by that?"

"He meant your ideas are certifiable—you know, the kind that you hang on the wall with a certificate of honor," Doc grinned.

Bud added, "Don't worry, Howie. No matter what, you'll always be our beloved Rockabilly Mayor. Now, let's go see if any wingwalkers transfer from plane to plane or hang by their teeth, like in the old days of wingwalker glory.

"Highly unlikely," Doc said as they set off for the runway.

35

It was late evening, and Bud sat in the living room at the Melon View B&B talking to Doc and Millie, who had just returned from dinner at the Willows.

He was tired and just wanted to go home, but he needed to find Scratch and ask him a few final questions, for Molly had called and said he and Joey were leaving by bus the next morning for Nebraska.

He suspected that Scratch had some of the answers he so desperately needed to make sense of things, yet he was worried that he could be barking up the wrong tree. Molly had said Scratch and Joey were out late doing some final chores for Kale, who had agreed to pay for their bus tickets in return, and she would send them Bud's way when they came in.

Bud was wondering what to do about Joey's thievery, not really sure he wanted to let him get on a bus and leave scot free, and yet he knew, as a minor, there wouldn't be a lot he could do except send him to the juvenile court up in Price. He suspected nothing much would come from that, given the petty nature of what had been stolen. It might be better to just let him leave.

Doc and Millie had finally said goodnight, and Bud was about to give up on seeing Scratch and Joey, when the door opened and

Hawk came in. He nodded to Bud, then quickly headed for the stairs.

As he walked by, Bud said softly, "I have something of yours."

Looking uncertain, Hawk stopped, saying, "I haven't lost anything."

Bud now said, "Firmum in vita nihil."

Hawk replied, "You have the painting, don't you? Good work. Where is it?"

Taken aback, Bud was silent for a moment, then said, "How do I know it's really yours?"

"I can produce a receipt, plus a statement from the museum. Kate has no claim to it. Sheriff Shumway, it's a civil case, not a criminal one, and not in your jurisdiction. Now then, where is it?"

"It's just like you told me, isn't it?" Bud replied. "Liars and thieves, except I have no idea at this point which is which. But I wasn't referring to the painting when I said I have something of yours."

"I never said anything about liars and thieves, though it's true," Hawk replied. "What could you possibly have besides the painting?"

"Tad, what were you doing in Black Dragon Cave with Ted Henderson?" Bud asked. He thought he could see the little bit of Hawk's face that wasn't concealed turn white.

"My name is Hawk. Why would you think I was in the cave?" Hawk replied.

"I found your ring there, the one you used to seal the letter you sent me. Do you care to talk about it? I would really appreciate some clarification, though I'm beginning to think I see the pieces of the puzzle falling together."

Hawk replied, "No crime has been committed. I would like to have the ring back. It has a long family history."

"You can come by my office tomorrow and get it," Bud replied. Now hearing Scratch's voice at the kitchen door, he added, "After you answer a few questions. You have nothing to fear if no crime has been committed."

"I'll pick up the painting then, too," Hawk added, now heading for the stairs as Scratch and Joey came into the room.

The pair looked tired, but happy.

"We're leaving in the morning, Sheriff," Scratch said. "Joey's family has invited me to come visit them. They have a farm, and they said I can work for them until I can get things going otherwise."

"What would that 'otherwise' entail?" Bud asked.

Joey answered, "My dad works for the county, and he says they have some housing available for old folks—not that Scratch is really old, he just kind of looks that way."

Giving Joey a look, Scratch replied, "I qualify. I'm 67. Old enough."

"That's great," Bud said. "Have either of you ever been to Nebraska?"

"Lots of times to visit my grandparents," Joey said. "Scratch will like it just fine."

"I hope so," Bud said. "But I really need to ask you guys some questions before you leave."

"Ask away," Joey replied.

"OK," Bud said. "Scratch, you said you saw a fellow out there in the canyons taking photos, but you didn't know who he was, then later you said you'd been drinking tea with some guy you knew. Was that guy one and the same person? Was his name Ted Henderson by any chance?"

Scratch, looking contrite, said, "Yes, Sheriff, it was Ted. He was the guy bringing me food. We got to be good friends. I don't know why I lied about it. I guess I was scared."

"Scared of what?" Bud asked.

"You know, that I'd be blamed for his death."

"Can you tell me more about that, Scratch?"

"Well, like I said, he and I got to be good friends. We were on the same wavelength, so to speak. We both had an interest in the mysteries of the universe. He'd come out and take night photos, and we'd build a nice fire and eat the food he'd brought, then talk into the wee hours."

"Go on," Bud encouraged.

"Well, Ted was a pretty straight shooter, but one night, I made me a nice brew of Jimson tea."

"What's that?" Joey asked.

"Don't you ever go trying it," Scratch said with concern. "It's deadly poison if you don't know what you're doing."

"Datura?" Bud asked.

"Yup, Datura. Jimsonweed. Moonflower. I know exactly how much to use to get a little mystical, which I liked to do once in awhile. You boil the leaves. It frees the spirit and mind. You can travel without ever going anywhere—physically, anyway. So, one night, Ted decided he wanted to try it. It's an hallucinogen, you know, and it deeply affected him. I had to sit all night with him. He scared me to death, thinking he wasn't going to recover, but he finally went to sleep and was able to go home the next day."

Scratch paused, then continued. "He didn't come back out for awhile, and I was getting pretty worried, as well as pretty hungry, but he finally came back, and we did it again, but this time I reduced the dose because he was more sensitive to it than me, not having done it as much."

"Did this become a regular thing?" Bud asked.

"Yes, it did. He was the only reason I was able to survive out there. We had some fantastic conversations, I can tell you. I miss him."

Scratch now stopped, as if reminiscing.

Bud said, "Go on, Scratch. I need to know how he died."

"I had nothing to do with that," Scratch said in his defense. "Well, maybe I did from starting him on the tea, but he went too far with it. Apparently he met some guy who claimed to be a famous artist. There was some kind of artsy thing going on there in town. Ted talked too much sometimes, and this was one of those times—he was a real friendly person. This artist guy was intrigued by Ted's stories about seeing starry skies like no one had ever seen before, that kind of thing. The artist said he was a fan of Vincent van Gogh and wanted to see the world as the artist had seen it. He told us that Van Gogh had lead poisoning from the paint everyone used back then and had visions, which is why he had such a swirly technique. Next thing I knew, this guy was here in the canyon for some tea over a fire, if you get my drift."

"What was this guy's name?" Bud asked.

"You know, I never did get it, partly because it was a one night thing, then everyone was gone. Ted was dead and this other guy never came back."

"What happened?" Joey asked.

"Well, I brewed up some tea, even though I can say I didn't feel real comfortable doing it with a stranger there. I didn't like the responsibility. I didn't even drink any, like maybe I had a premonition that something bad was going to happen. I had no idea how this guy would react, and Jimson can make a person real volatile, and sure enough, both of them got going and didn't stop when they should have. They got into some kind of argument over what true art was, of all things, and when I realized how much tea they'd been drinking, I felt sick. Jimsonweed can be fatal with enough of a dose."

Now Scratch looked as if he was about to cry.

"I feel responsible, yet they drank of their own accord. I tried to get them to stop. This guy picked up a stick and attacked me, saying I'd cut off Van Gogh's ear. Ted threw his camera at him to get him to stop. That's actually how I hurt my hand, not trying to catch the drone."

Scratch continued. "When I realized how bad things were getting, I dumped out the tea and left. I know the canyons like the back of my hand, and I went and hid in Black Dragon Cave. I fell asleep, only to wake to Ted crawling in. He knew I slept in there sometimes. He was crying and carrying on, saying he was dying. I tried to comfort him, and that other fellow, he must have heard us, because he crawled in, too. At that point, I guess we all passed out. When I woke, it was morning, and the artist guy was gone, and so was Ted, but in another way, a bad way. He was dead."

Now Scratch was weeping, Joey patting him on the back. He finally got ahold of himself and said, "I hightailed it over to Double Arch Canyon, which is where I usually stayed in an alcove, as there's water there. I didn't know what to do. Next thing I knew, these people were in there pushing each other around, and one guy fell off a rock.

The others left, and by the time I'd gotten down there, the guy who'd fallen was gone, too."

"Did you see who pushed him?" Bud asked.

"I think it was a woman," Scratch replied. "But I got a little ahead of myself, Sheriff. The day before this artist guy came out for some tea, Ted had been in the canyon taking pictures with his camera and his drone. He said someone had come out and buried something and he had it on video, but they'd crashed his drone with rocks and he couldn't find it. I found it later, but I left it there."

"I'm confused, Scratch. These people came out and dug a grave, then this friend of Ted's came out that night and drank tea?"

"Yes, that's right. Then the next day, these people came out and were pushing each other around."

"Is it possible that it was all the same people both days?"

"Yes, very possible."

"And that the guy that was pushed was also the artist guy who drank tea with you and Ted?"

"Yes, he did look the same, though it was kind of too far to be sure. That same day, I saw you and some other guy come out, then the ambulance took Ted away."

Bud said, "It's starting to make sense, Scratch. It's late, and you guys have to get up really early, as the bus leaves at 5 a.m. Have you seen anyone around here that could match who you saw in the canyons?"

Scratch replied, "No, but I'm never inside here, Sheriff. Before we all part ways, I want to tell you I really appreciate everything you've done for me."

Joey added, "Me, too, Sheriff. I know what I did was wrong, and I'm going to send money to everyone I stole from. It might not be much, but I already have a job working for my uncle when I get out there."

"That would be a good thing, Joey," Bud replied, standing to go. "Otherwise, you wouldn't be very welcome to come back, and it's never wise to burn one's bridges. But I have one more question for you, Scratch. Would you mind telling me your real name?"

"Sure," Scratch said. "It's Ted—Ted Miles."

Bud shook his head at the improbability, said goodnight, and was soon on his way home, wondering what the next day would bring.

36

It was early, and Bud was in his office, drinking coffee, cruising the Internet, searching for information on the RC show, wondering when it ended. Out of curiosity, he got sidetracked and searched on Black Dragon Canyon.

> *Black Dragon is a perfect name. Hidden away, this amazing canyon looks as if a dragon has burned it over and over with its fiery breath! It is breathtaking. Be sure to find the petroglyphs—they are beautiful.*

Bud smiled, recalling the many times he'd gone into the canyon just to get away and enjoy nature. Of course, this was before Ted Henderson had overdosed himself on Jimsonweed, and he knew he would always think of him from now on when he went there.

Bud now pulled up an article titled, *Archaeological Interpretations of the Black Dragon Pictograph.*

> *Years ago, someone outlined the pictograph in white chalk, outlining pigmented areas, but also including areas that were not colored. When archaeologists in the Barrier Canyon style of pictographs and petroglyphs*

looked at the panel, they saw five separate figures, not one dragon. Two techniques were used to examine the panel.

Dstretch is a digital imaging tool designed to enhance photographs of pictographs. It will reveal pigments faded to the point that they are no longer visible to the human eye. X-ray fluorescence measures the iron concentration in red pigment to show pigment on rock surfaces. Both of these techniques showed that the Black Dragon Panel is actually five separate pictographs. On the left are two small figures, a bighorn sheep and a dog. Next is a large, bug-eyed anthropomorph with a snake in its hand. Further to the right is the figure of a man, bent at the waist with arms outstretched in supplication. The last figure to the right is a large, sinuous horned snake. All five figures are Barrier Canyon Style, from 4,000 to 1,500 years ago, and named for a series of rock art panels along Barrier Creek, just 45 miles away.

Bud leaned back. He'd been right in suspecting something was off with the dragon—it wasn't a dragon at all! Just like everything else lately, it was an illusion, all mixed up and confused.

He was now pretty sure that, like Hawk had said, no crime had been committed, though he had a few loose ends to tie up, namely talking again to Charles and Kate, as well as to Tad AKA Hawk. He hoped he could catch them all before they left town, as he knew the silent auction was coming soon, which would end the festival.

He wondered if Tad would actually come into his office, like he'd said he would the previous evening. If he did, he wasn't really sure what to do with the painting at this point. He knew he still needed to talk to Kate one more time and get her perspective before releasing it to anyone.

Just then, his office door opened and Tad walked in. Not having actually ever met him when he wasn't posing as Hawk, Bud wasn't sure at first who it was, but upon seeing a trace of black marker on his upper lip, as well as on his eyebrows, Bud asked, "What happened to Hawk?"

Tad replied, "In the words of the great philosopher Emile Zola, *Le passé n'était que le cimetière de nos illusions, on s'y brisait les pieds contre des tombes."*

Bud replied, "My French is a little rusty these days, not ever having studied it."

Tad said, "The past is but the cemetery of our illusions, one simply stubs one's toes on the gravestones."

"So, you're saying Hawk was but an illusion? Or was he a gravestone?"

Tad laughed. "He was a necessary evil. Now, the painting, please."

Ignoring his request, Bud said, "You must have had quite an experience out in Black Dragon with Ted and Scratch."

"How do you know about that?"

"Scratch told me."

Tad sighed, then said, "Yes, it's changed my life. The universe informed me I was on the wrong track and needed correction. I know now that I am simply like the hawkmoth to the beautiful Datura flower, just a necessary imposition."

"I don't understand," Bud said.

"As a non-artist, you're probably not aware that I have a reputation in the art world. My paintings sell for many hundreds of thousands of dollars. I'm represented in many prestigious museums and galleries. I've made it my life to create art. I admire Van Gogh immensely, as he created what I call pure art—art with no motive other than to just create. Quoting the great Zola once again, *Une oeuvre d'art est un coin de la création vu à travers un tempérament.* A work of art is a corner of creation seen through a temperament.' My temperament has been controversial, but successful."

"And is Charles also a Van Gogh fan?" Bud asked.

"Only because Kate is and he wants to impress her. *I* am the original Van Gogh fan. But quite frankly, I'm a pain in the rear of the art world. My stuff sells well, but I've always been overly critical of others. A lot of people hate me, including Kate. My night in Black Dragon taught me that I must be more generous. I'm trying hard, believe me."

"When did you realize Ted Henderson was dead?"

"I had no idea Ted was dead until I heard about his service, which I attended. When I left the cave, I assumed he was still alive."

"And you attended that service as Hawk."

"Yes, out of necessity. I couldn't be seen there. But I felt very bad for him. I saw Kate and Charles there and felt a sense of satisfaction, knowing they believed Ted was me. Like a lot of people, they didn't pay attention."

Bud thought back to what Doc had said about schadenfreude as he watched Hawk at the service.

He said, "You seemed to be enjoying their reaction."

"I won't deny it. They thought they'd killed me and were terrified they'd be arrested, yet they were glad I was gone. I enjoyed seeing how they acted. It was like attending my own funeral, though they had the wrong guy."

"Then Kate was the one who pushed you off the rock?"

Tad looked surprised. "You know about that? Yes, it was Kate. I still haven't decided if it was something she would do at any time or if it was in the heat of the moment. But I don't really blame her. Datura can take up to 48 hours to wear off. I left the cave the morning after we drank the tea, still hallucinating somewhat, Ted and Scratch still sleeping, or so I thought. I went back to the B&B, and I was still feeling at odds and got into an argument with Charles. I took my stuff and left, and followed them back to the canyon where they were painting. We again got into a bit of a scuffle, I'm afraid. The fall knocked the wind out of me, but I soon got up and was able to leave in my car."

Tad continued. "I was going to go back to the B&B, but I had wondered all along if Kate didn't want me dead, which is why I sent you the letter in the first place. I decided to go back in disguise. That way I could spy on them and see which way to take things. I knew they had the painting. They took it from my house."

"And you don't want to have them arrested for theft?"

"No, I just want the painting back. But I will admit I enjoyed spying on them and torturing Kate with my silly additions to the community painting. She had to know it was me from my style. She must've thought I was communing from beyond the grave."

"She did," Bud replied. "I got word of each change from Molly. But that's why you sent me the cryptic letter, you were afraid of being killed?" Bud asked.

Tad replied, "Well, I'm not totally surprised you figured out it was me. I sent that letter because I thought they were out to get me, especially after I realized I still had Kate on my insurance policy."

Bud thought back to how upset Kate had been that Tad had remarried, even though she'd been confusing him with Ted Henderson.

"Why not change it?" Bud asked.

"I actually did, but I never got the chance to tell her. You have a reputation, Sheriff, and I knew if I sent you that letter, you'd start probing into things if I was killed."

Bud replied, "I would've done that anyway."

"I was hoping maybe you'd start investigating *before* I was killed and somehow prevent it. I did think they would kill me, but now I'm not so sure Kate actually meant to push me off the cliff. We got kind of tangled up, and I'm sure she just reacted, thinking I was going to push her off."

"Why didn't you just come to me in the first place?" Bud asked. "Or better yet, just stay away from them?"

Tad replied, "All I had was suspicion. And like I said, the old me, the me before Black Dragon, enjoyed drama. My entire art career has been founded on it. I knew I should stay far away from them, but I'd already planned this plein air thing. And I entertained myself quite well learning how to letterlock—it's quite the science—and then writing that letter. Now can I have my ring back?"

"So the way you sealed the letter is called letterlocking?" Bud asked.

Tad replied, "Yes, letterlocking is a very old technique, one used especially by people like Mary Queen of Scots to pass secret communications. It's an art where one folds and secures a letter, making it function as its own envelope. There are lots of different ways to do it, and all are quite difficult to master. I'm a master at it now."

As Tad was talking, Bud took the ring from his desk drawer and handed it to him.

"That ring's worth a fortune, and you kept it in your desk? Sacrilege!"

"At least I didn't lose it in some remote canyon. But are you wanting to press charges against Charles or Kate? Charles did push you into the fireplace at the B&B, according to Molly. And Kate pushed you off the rock, whether intentional or not."

"Well, Sheriff, the old Tad would have definitely filed charges, as well as gotten a top-notch attorney. But the hawkmoth says no."

"Do you mind telling me more about what kind of transformation you've had? If it's too personal, I understand."

Tad replied, "No, it's fine. Like I said, the universe decided to give me a second chance. I've been transformed from an arrogant know-it-all to the humble hawkmoth who lives as a conduit for beauty. See, the hawkmoth pollinates the beautiful Datura, allowing it to show-case its beauty to the entire world. The hawkmoth is happy staying behind the scenes."

Tad paused, and Bud was beginning to think he was done, but he continued. "That night, I saw the world as Van Gogh must've seen it in all its beauty. Black Dragon Canyon is a place that will always be special to me, even though Ted died there. I've adopted the hawk-moth as my avatar to remind me of who I am. The hawkmoth symbolizes rebirth, transformation, and the power of regeneration in Native American mythology. In fact, butterflies and moths both hold a significant position in many native cultures. Did you think my choice of a last name was clever?"

"You mean Papillon? It's kind of hard to pronounce," Bud replied.

"It's French for moth or butterfly."

"Nice," Bud replied. "But Scratch said you told them that Van Gogh was poisoned by lead paint and that's why he saw things."

"That's true, but who's to say that what he saw wasn't the real world and what we think we see is but an illusion? Some people are happy living in an illusion. As someone once said, madness is in the world, not in us."

"Someone also once said that the word *swims* upside-down is still *swims*," Bud replied. "But Tad, did Kate and Charles even stop to see if you were dead or alive?"

"I was out of it, Sheriff. I not only was still feeling the effects of the Datura, but I'd had the wind knocked out of me. I don't remember. But what do you mean about the word *swims*? I don't get it."

"I'm just saying that I believe the world exists independent of what we think or perceive. My friend Howie has taught me to look at things from a more scientific perspective, but we're all entitled to our own opinions."

"Maybe true, but what about my painting? Can I get it back now?"

"Have you considered that maybe it's an illusion and doesn't actually exist?" Bud asked.

Tad groaned as Bud added, "I want to talk to Kate first and get her story. I can't just release it to you without doing that. I'm sure you understand, being a reasonable person now and all that."

Bud stood and put on his jacket, adding, "And now it's time for me to lock up and go have some lunch, as my stomach has the illusion that it's starving. Why don't you join me? But one last question—are you really from Sego?"

Tad shook his head no as Bud showed him the door, and they both headed for the Melon Rind Cafe.

37

As Bud and Tad approached the cafe, Bud's cell phone rang, and he could tell from the caller ID it was Wilma Jean.

"Yell-ow."

"Hon, there are two guys here at the cafe, and they've been hanging around the front door for a good half-hour, filming people and interviewing them, and when I asked them what they were doing, they said they needed to get an invitation from you before they could come inside. Do you have any idea what's going on?"

Bud laughed. "I'm almost there. I'll take care of it."

As they reached the door of the cafe, Bud said, "Hello fellas. You have my invitation to come on in."

The guy with the camera, seeing Tad, said, "Tad Hall! Remember me? That documentary on BBC about Van Gogh?"

Tad grinned, then replied, "Of course I remember you, Will. But quite frankly, I'm surprised you'll still talk to me. My apologies for all that." Tad shook the guy's hand.

"What are you doing in Green River, Utah?" Will the cameraman asked.

"I was going to ask you the same thing," Tad replied. "There's a plein air festival here."

"Man, this little town has everything," Will said. "A neat museum, river trips, a watermelon float, rafting, famous artists, and cafes where you eat by invitation only."

Bud grinned, leaving Tad with the two fellows and going to his back booth.

Wilma Jean was soon there with a cup of coffee, sitting down across from him.

"Hon, what was that all about?" She asked.

"I honestly don't know, except those two guys wanted to film in the cafe and I told them no, it was private, by invitation only."

"Good call," she replied. "At least until we know what they're going to do with it. But next time, tell them the owner, which would be me, can also issue invitations. I told them to come in, but they said no, you were the one who did the invites. But what's the big hoopla?"

"That's Tad Hall, famous artist. Surely you've heard of him?"

"No."

"Me, neither."

"Why are they filming everything?"

"I have no idea."

As Will the cameraman began taking his camera from its case, he noticed Bud watching and nodded for them to go outside, where they then appeared to be interviewing Tad on film. Wilma Jean, seeing what was going on, ran out, and Bud could see she was instructing them to turn around and film so the cafe's sign would be shown.

He grinned—his wife would make a good director, he figured—a good *film* director, he corrected himself, since she already pretty much directed him around. He watched as she stopped and talked to the trio for a moment, then came back inside.

"They're making some kind of travel show about Green River," she told Bud. "I told them to be sure to come to Rockabilly Night tomorrow. It's right after the plein air show and silent auction."

"Did you mention Eileen and Frosty's wedding? That should be filmworthy."

"I didn't tell you? They decided to elope. They're going to Las Vegas. Eileen wants an Elvis wedding."

"Seriously? After all that work we did at the rehearsal?"

Wilma Jean laughed. "I think that rehearsal is what made them decide to go to Vegas."

Bud sighed, glad to be off the hook. "I guess it's OK, as long as they don't stay at the Heartbreak Hotel."

"I expected you to say something corny like that, hon, but I thought it would be something more like them being all shook up or something to do with hound dogs."

"We'll still have the buffet, won't we?" He asked hopefully.

"No buffet, and I can't say I'm sad about that. I need a break."

"Shoots," Bud replied. "I was really looking forward to it. But wait! The plein air festival's almost over?"

"Tomorrow's the last day."

"Just what does plein air mean, anyway?" Bud asked.

"En plein air—French for *outside*," Doc said, walking through the door.

"Doc!" Bud said. "I've been wondering where you were. It seems like everyone's leaving. Are you guys going to be here for awhile longer?"

"I think we're leaving day after tomorrow, Bud. We want to go to Rockabilly Night."

"I need to talk to Kate and Charles before they leave," Bud said. "But Doc, I think I've made some headway on everything, finally. I had a nice talk with Scratch, and also Hawk, who actually is Tad."

"Is that him talking outside? I heard them mention something about a show on Green River. Who are they with, anyway?"

"I don't know, but Tad knows them."

"Bud, Millie's out in the Rover. We're on our way to the River Museum. We heard they've judged the plein air show entrants. Do you want to go along with us?"

"Sure," Bud replied, gathering up his jacket. "I'll follow you there."

Wilma Jean, who had gone back behind the counter, said, "Doc, you and Millie are invited to dinner tonight. Seven o'clock give or take an hour. Don't be late."

Doc laughed, saying, "It's hard to be late with a timeframe like that. We'll see you then."

They were soon at the museum, wandering around looking at the entrants, most available for the silent auction the next day. A number of people Bud recognized from the B&B were there, as well as locals and people Bud assumed were tourists.

The show was organized so that one started with the paintings that had received no awards, then worked their way from those receiving an honorable mention to those that placed third, second, and first, then eventually to the Best of Show and People's Choice awards.

As they slowly made the rounds, Doc said, "Since Van Gogh seems to be the talk du jour, did you know that he was known to paint en plein air even on windy days? A number of his paintings have grains of sand embedded in their surface."

"Interesting," Bud replied. "Especially since I didn't even know he was a plein air painter."

"Oh my, look at this one," Millie said. They had worked their way to the honorable mention paintings, and she stood admiring an impressionistic painting with oranges and reds that was titled, *Pastel Geyser Glow*.

"Must be the Green River Geyser," Doc said. "Though it looks more to me like what's left after two RC airplanes crash."

Millie, giving Doc a look, replied, "It's obviously supposed to be the colors in the travertine, silly. It's by Kate Meadows, one of the B&B guests."

"Didn't her husband say this was her first show?" Bud asked. "It's a lot better than I could do."

They wandered on, examining the third-place entry, a scene of white egrets on the river called *Rejoice*; the second-place entry, a painting of the desert with railroad tracks in the foreground and the Bookcliffs in the background called *Looking North at Mount Elliot*; and the first-place entry, a very realistic painting of the old Fruitgrowers Bank called *Times Past*.

After admiring them all, they finally reached the Best of Show, which was also the People's Choice, a large painting of beautiful creamy datura blooms with pale purple highlights and colorful hawkmoths hovering over them, all set in a deep canyon with blue-bird skies over a double arch. On one wall was the Black Dragon petroglyph. It was called, simply, *Paradise Found*.

"Mill, I think we should bid on this one. It's stunning," Doc said.

"Except it says it's not for sale, dear," Millie replied. "Who's the artist?"

Bud leaned down to read the signature in the corner. "It's by Tad Hall."

"He's very talented," Millie said. "I would love to hang this in our living room."

"Well, everything has a price, dear," Doc said. "Though I doubt if we could afford what it would take to buy this one."

Now a man's voice behind them said, "Your Sheriff friend here has something I would gladly trade for that painting, if you could just convince him."

There stood Tad himself, to Bud's chagrin.

38

"Tad, your paintings probably sell for more than that Van Gogh is worth," Bud replied. "Why not just sell this one and buy another Van Gogh? Then you and Kate will both have one."

Tad gave Bud an icy look, then said, "I don't have time for the trouble. I want my original back."

"Good lord! You have an original Van Gogh?" Millie asked.

"It looks like an original, but it's actually a 3D copy from the museum," Bud countered. "They have more like it for sale."

Tad, now looking irritated, said, "Sheriff, that painting belongs to me. I can prove it."

"Interesting," Bud replied. "I thought I saw a hawkmoth on your shoulder for the briefest moment. It appears to have flown away."

Tad, looking irritated, shrugged his shoulders.

"I'm kind of lost here," Doc said. "Is this painting for sale or not?"

Bud replied, "I guess you can try to negotiate with the artist, but I need to go out to the B&B and talk to someone. I really enjoyed our little artwalk, especially seeing how art-illiterate I am, but I'm learning more every day. I'll catch up with you all later at dinner. And Tad, you're welcome to come, too. Doc can give you directions, and just in case it crossed your mind, the painting's not at my house, but is hidden somewhere else in a safe."

As Bud started to leave, Tad pleaded, "Sheriff, California property law disallows title to stolen goods. You can't give it back to Kate. The way they buried it in a grave shows how well they'll take care of it."

"Tad, you live in Nevada, and California laws don't apply there. I don't yet know who's getting that painting, but I can assure you it will be somewhere safe until you guys can settle this—legally. And be sure you're not wanting it back just to spite Kate, as that won't go down well if it goes to court."

Bud touched his hat and was soon on his way to the Melon View B&B. He first swung by his office and got the urn with the ashes and the black plastic bag full of dog toys, then headed out to the Melon View, hoping Charles and Kate were there.

He knew he was running out of time, as he figured most everyone would leave after the silent auction tomorrow, although some might stay for Rockabilly Night.

The place seemed unnaturally quiet, especially with Scratch and Joey gone, as he knew they'd left early that morning on the bus. Molly's car was gone, and he could see Kale way across the field on a tractor, which made him feel a touch of envy, for he was missing the peace and quiet that went with farming.

Pulling up to the parking area, he was glad to see the car with the California plates was there, which he knew was Charles and Kate's. It had a light yellow dusting of sand, which he knew was from Black Dragon Canyon, as well as mud up under the wheel wells.

Hesitant, now wondering if they would talk to him, given how they'd zoomed right past him out at the canyon's gate, he went on into the B&B.

He suddenly realized he had no idea which room they were in, and with Molly gone, he had no way of finding out, so he sat on the big overstuffed couch and picked up a nearby magazine. He would wait for awhile and see if they came out.

It was an old issue of *Outdoor Photography*, and Bud opened it, thinking it looked familiar. The first article was about how to photograph volcanoes, and he instantly knew it was one of a stack that had mysteriously disappeared from the coffee table at the bungalow, most of which he'd collected from the library's free box.

So, Wilma Jean had appropriated them, recycling them for B&B guests, Bud mused. Funny thing was, he hadn't even noticed they were gone.

He flipped through another, looking at an article on photographing rainbows, then decided to go in the kitchen and see if he could round up a cup of coffee. Just then, he heard what sounded like people arguing upstairs.

Abandoning the coffee idea, he walked to the base of the stairs and listened.

"Kate, forget the Van Gogh. It's time to go. I saw Tad at the art show, and he's definitely not dead."

"It's impossible! We saw him dead in the canyon ourselves. We went to his memorial. He can't be alive."

It sounded to Bud like Kate and Charles. He could hear their door open, and as they came down the hall, Kate said, "Be quiet. Some-one's going to hear us."

Seeing Bud standing at the bottom of the stairs, she added, "Someone *has* heard us."

"Come on down," Bud said. "I think I have your dog."

Now he could see Charles standing next to Kate, both looking down on him.

Kate replied, "You have our dog? Our dogs are at home. My dad's taking care of them."

"Black Dragon," Bud said. "Come on down."

Kate and Charles both hurried down the stairs, and Bud invited them to sit down. He then handed them the urn and bag of toys.

"His ashes!" Charles said. "And his toys and blankee. How did you get them?"

"I'm the one who dug up the grave," Bud said. "Out in Black Dragon Canyon."

"But why?" Kate asked.

"It's a long story, but I'll just say it had to do with investigating a death out there," Bud replied. "One you reported."

"But Charles said he saw Tad at the art show," Kate said. "He's not dead. We didn't kill him."

"Maybe you should add the words 'after all' to that sentence," Bud replied. "I could maybe be convinced you didn't mean to try to kill him, but only you know. But no, he wasn't dead when you found his body. He survived, no thanks to you two. You didn't even bother to check on him, nor did you tell me the whole story of what happened, but pretended to not know."

"He was pushing me, and I pushed back, Sheriff," Kate pleaded. "You have to believe me."

"Does this mean you also have the painting?" Charles asked.

"I do," Bud said. "And Tad knows I have it. He wants it back, but I don't feel qualified to make that judgement call. Maybe you can help me out with some facts."

Kate and Charles looked at each other, then Charles said, "It belongs to Kate."

"Why not start by telling me about your dog and why you buried him in the canyon? We can take it from there," Bud said.

"Black Dragon was an American Alsatian," Kate said.

"What's that?" Bud asked.

Charles replied, "It's a fairly new dog breed. They bred Alaskan Malamutes to German Shepherds, trying to get a dog that looks like a wolf yet that has the temperament of a domestic dog. It's a large breed that weighs around 100 pounds. The breeder wanted to recreate the extinct dire wolf look."

"And your dog was named Black Dragon?" Bud asked.

Kate answered, "Yes, that was the breeder's name for the puppy because he was exceptionally black, but we just called him Dragon."

"Did you come here just to bury him in the canyon?" Bud asked.

She continued. "No, we had already booked the B&B and the plein air event before Dragon died. He died just before we came out here, and Charles saw it on a map and decided it would be appropriate to bury his ashes in a canyon with his name. I was very upset by it all, as he was my best friend. I'd had him since he was a puppy, and I spent a lot of money on him, though that really didn't matter. We have two other dogs at home. My dad's taking care of them."

"We noticed you seemed to be on edge," Bud said.

"Yes, I've been an emotional wreck. First, I'd lost my best friend, Dragon, then I found out my ex-husband, Tad, was also staying at the B&B. Keep in mind that Charles had just gone into Tad's house and taken the Van Gogh."

"Charles actually stole the painting?"

"Yes—no—I don't know. Is it stealing to get something back that belongs to you? Tad agreed for me to have the painting in the divorce, then reneged on it just to spite me. He didn't even really want it. Charles and I have known each other for years, and we got married right after the divorce. I waited a year for Tad to give the painting back, and he didn't, so Charles got really angry and went and got it. Tad didn't even try to stop him, just watched him do it, knowing he could call the police and get Charles in trouble. But the divorce settlement says it's mine, so who knows what's going to happen?"

"But why bury something so valuable?" Bud asked.

"We wrapped it really well and intended to come back and get it after all this blew over. We were trying to protect Charles. If he didn't have the painting, how could Tad prove he'd taken it? It was his word against Charles'."

"You were going to come back and dig up the grave later?"

"At first, we were going to just come back and dig up the painting later, but then I decided I didn't want Dragon out in that desolate canyon. We weren't sure if it was legal or not to bury a dog on public land, that's why we said we hadn't been in Black Dragon Canyon. We decided to get his ashes and the painting, and put his ashes in my rose bushes back home. We went out to get everything, but someone had taken it all. I suspected Tad had somehow figured out where we hid it. I can't tell you how upset that made me."

"So what about the communal painting at the B&B? Did you suspect Tad was still alive and tormenting you by painting symbolic stuff while no one was looking?"

"I hadn't figured that one out yet. I really thought he was dead, but it was his style on the painting. I was very upset at that point over the entire thing."

"Can you tell me what really happened in Double Arch Canyon?" Bud asked.

Kate said, "After the altercation at the B&B, Tad followed us into Double Arch Canyon and demanded we give the painting back. We'd climbed a ways up into some rocks at that point, looking for a good place to paint. Tad and Charles started pushing each other around, and I got involved, trying to stop them, and accidentally pushed Tad off a rock. I can't tell you how close I came to getting pushed off that same rock by him, so I felt I acted in self-defense. He was acting so terribly odd, not at all like himself. But I truly thought I'd killed him. I'm not a murderer, Mr. Shumway, and Charles and I thought he was dead. So we quickly went to your office. We didn't want his body left out there, but we also didn't want to be accused of murder."

"And you had buried your dog the previous day, right? Were you aware that the burial had been captured by a drone camera?"

"We weren't sure. Charles said he heard something, and when he actually saw the drone, we threw rocks at it. We hit it, and we then hurried and got out of there."

"Did you see anyone else in there?"

"We did. There was a guy with a camera on a tripod, taking photos, but he was on the other side of the canyon from us."

"Was he a big guy?"

"It was hard to tell, but we passed an old blue pickup that might have been his."

Bud stopped to think, fiddling with his harmonica, then asked, "So, you buried your dog in Black Dragon, saw Ted Henderson, who filmed you burying it, went back to the B&B, then went back to Double Arch Canyon the next day to paint after the argument with Tad."

"That's right," Charles replied.

Bud continued. "You didn't know that Tad had spent the previous night in Black Dragon, drinking Datura tea with Ted Henderson, the photographer guy whose memorial you attended?"

"How would we know that?" Kate asked.

Bud replied, "Tad went back to the B&B the next morning, still somewhat affected by the hallucinogen, got into a fight with Charles, then followed you back out."

"It's very complicated, isn't it, Sheriff?" Charles said. "And so, this other guy, the photographer who filmed us burying Dragon, was the one who actually died? What did he die from?"

Bud replied, "He overdosed on Datura, a poisonous plant that grows in the canyons. But didn't you ever wonder about all the discrepancies about Tad's death? For example, the memorial service and the fact that he had a wife and house in Green River?"

Kate replied, "I wondered many times, but I figured he was just very devious, living a hidden life and changing his last name. He'd fooled me with his behavior before, doing things I had no idea about."

"That drone footage was what allowed me to see what you guys were doing," Bud said. "But one last thing. Had you considered killing Tad for his life insurance, which you may have thought was still in your name? There is some evidence that leans toward that, like when you were upset because you heard he'd remarried."

Kate looked horrified. "No! I would never kill anyone. You have to believe me. I was upset because he's left everything to our children, as far as I know, and I worried that a new wife might muddle things up."

"Kate is very protective of her kids," Charles added. "She's like a momma bear. Just like with her dogs."

Bud thought for a moment, then said, "Well, I'm now pretty convinced that no crime was committed, unless you or Tad want to press some kind of charges for pushing each other around, but I don't think any of you would have much of a case at this point. Ted Henderson's overdose was accidental. I have the painting in my safe, and I think it's going to stay there until this is all settled in court, which may be awhile."

He added, "I'm going to go make some coffee, if you want some.

And congrats on your geyser painting, by the way, Kate. It's quite nice."

"Congratulations? For what?"

"It made honorable mention, which is pretty good, considering the competition," Bud replied.

"It did?" Kate seemed shocked.

"I told you," said Charles. "You have a lot of talent, but you won't believe me. But let's go to the museum."

"Just be aware that Tad may still be there," Bud advised. "And you do know he's back at the B&B here, don't you?"

"I swore I saw him, but Kate said I had to be mistaken. He was that Hawk guy all along, wasn't he? But we're leaving soon, so we'll be able to avoid him until then, I'm sure. Thanks for your help, Sheriff," Charles said.

"Anytime," Bud replied, heading for the kitchen, wondering what he'd done that they would thank him for, other than digging up their dog's grave and returning its ashes to them.

He shrugged his shoulders and started a pot of that delicious coffee Wilma Jean had ordered from Wicked Brew, figuring he might just hide out at the B&B for awhile, since everyone else was in town. He'd eventually work up his courage, then stop by Rachael Henderson's and tell her how he'd royally mixed everything up, his only consolation being that he wasn't the only one.

39

It was the next day, and Bud had taken the dogs for a ride out in the Big Empty, happy it was his day off and he could get away for awhile, as the town seemed to be crawling with people.

Not only had some of the RC airplane people stayed, but all the plein air artists who had been out in the backcountry painting were now hanging around town, and even better, a spring ballgame was going on between the Green River Melonheads and a softball team from Price called the Carbonate Raptors.

He felt the Melonheads moniker was maybe a bit overboard, yet it seemed to fit, and the name Carbonate Raptors definitely fit a team from a coal mining town near a dinosaur quarry.

He was glad Doc and Millie wouldn't be leaving until the day after the rockabilly concert, yet he was kind of glad Doc had opted to go play more golf with Millie, for he was feeling the need to be alone. Wilma Jean was at the cafe, and Howie was at his drive-in, having called Bud that morning to make sure he was going to Rockabilly Night, as he said he had a big announcement to make.

Bud pulled the FJ over near a huge block of sandstone that had fallen from the cliffs high above many eons ago, a rock that he knew had been there a long time, as it had some faint petroglyphs on one side. It also provided some shade from the sun, which was beginning to blaze hotter and hotter, now that summer was around the corner.

He let the dogs out, who immediately began sniffing around the nearby rocks and shrubs, glad to have their freedom. He walked to the petroglyphs, which he'd discovered some years back on a similar foray.

The majority of petroglyphs and pictographs he'd seen in the canyons were in sheltered alcoves or on the north sides of rocks, which gave them protection from the sun, but these were in the direct sun, and the only reason they were still visible was that they were petroglyphs, pecked into the rocks instead of painted.

It was hard to make out what the artist had intended them to be, but it looked vaguely like several mountain sheep with big curly horns and a strange bird-like figure with outstretched wings.

He stood for a moment as a wave of recognition came over him. This birdlike thing looked exactly like the Black Dragon over in the canyon, some 30 miles or so distant, the one that had been shown to be five different figures chalked together.

But here he was, looking at the exact same thing, yet this one was definitely one figure, not a composite. It looked old, and he wondered if it had been the prototype for the one in Black Dragon Canyon. Had someone thousands of years ago created this figure, then another Native artist saw it and recreated it over in Black Dragon Canyon as a puzzle using different figures? Had someone taken it upon themselves to add their own mark of creativity to the original by making it a composite?

He knew there had to be a connection. Was this figure newer, modeled after the five petroglyphs in the canyon? Did the natives even have a concept of dragons? As far as he knew, no one had ever discovered one in the numerous drawings in the canyons.

Thinking back, Bud remembered Hawk telling him that things might seem complicated, even though they actually weren't. He knew he'd felt lately like everything was too complex to figure out, yet he knew that it was almost a choice one made of how to view the world

—as something complex yet with an underlying simplicity that governed how things worked.

Bud went back to the FJ and got his thermos, then sat down on a nearby rock and poured himself a cup of coffee. For a moment, he could feel the tautness of suspenders pulling against his chest, then laughed at himself. It was a residual memory, kind of like when one gets contacts and keeps trying to push their non-existent glasses up the bridge of their nose.

He didn't miss the suspenders, and he still found it kind of odd that they'd belonged to George. Wilma Jean seemed to have completely forgotten about them, for she'd never mentioned them again.

Coffee gone, he pulled his harmonica from his shirt pocket and began again trying to play *Springtime in the Rockies*, then gave up, putting it back in his pocket. Maybe it was time for a trip to the mountains, as they hadn't had a vacation for some time—maybe when the spring planting was done and Kale wouldn't need his help.

He leaned back, thinking of everything that had happened the past week or so, glad things had begun to make more sense.

It had been an odd feeling wondering why everything was so confusing, and he'd begun doubting his analytical abilities, but it seemed there had been a good reason for it, given the number of people named Ted and Tad and whatnot that he'd been dealing with. It had taught him to never make assumptions, a lesson he thought he'd already learned, but apparently not.

He pulled the perfect-crime letter from his pocket, thinking back to what seemed ages ago when he'd first read it. It still seemed odd to him, mysterious even, and he wasn't sure he would ever really understand it, other than as something from the mind of an eccentric artist.

> The perfect crime,
> Will soon be committed.
> You won't know it happened,
> No sleuthing permitted.
> There won't be a body,

No suspects, nor clues.
This letter you're holding,
Your only news.
Iris and wheatfields,
Starry skies filled with crows.
Missing ears and letters,
So life and death goes.
—Yer pal, Vinnie

Putting the letter away, he wondered if he was missing something, if perhaps the perfect crime *had* been committed and he would never know.

He then thought back to the phone call he'd received from Tad that morning saying he was officially returning the Van Gogh replica to Kate, and would Bud kindly give it to her? Bud hadn't known what to say, but he had called Kate, who'd come with Charles to get it.

Now sitting out in the wilds, far from other humans or civilization, Bud felt a sense of futility about it all, but in a good way. What did a painting matter out here to the lizards and canyon wrens and rabbitbrush and fishhook cacti? Nothing at all. It was of no significance, and that was how it should be. Just like the old cabin melting into the canyon that Scratch had called the Black Dragon Cafe, it was all temporary and ephemeral.

The dogs, now tired of chasing and sniffing, came to him, and he put a pan of water out for them. After drinking, they lay down at his feet, snoozing.

Now getting sleepy, Bud thought of Vincent van Gogh and wondered what his life had been like. He didn't know much about the artist, other than the bits and pieces he'd heard from others, but it seemed like his life had been tortured and too short, and yet he'd managed to create an abundance of beautiful artwork that had enhanced the lives of many people. Bud thought it was a shame the artist hadn't been able to see the wonder he'd brought to others through his creativity.

He now thought of his own creativity, and how he expressed it through his photography and even his harmonica, as minor as both seemed in the grand scheme of things. But that was OK, for what really mattered was that he could make the world a better place, as insignificant as it might seem, for nothing in life is permanent.

He began to doze off, but then remembered he'd promised Wilma Jean he'd be back in time to help her plant the petunias and mums she'd bought from the hardware store, who'd just gotten a shipment in, so he finally woke the dogs and gathered them up and headed back to town, happy that he'd been able to get away for even a short time.

And even though he wasn't a big rockabilly fan, he was actually looking forward to Rockabilly Night and Howie's big announcement, whatever it might be.

40

Bud tilted his camp chair back, holding onto the back of Wilma Jean's chair, enjoying the cool shade of the big maple trees in the city park. Across the grassy lawn, the big white Athena missile caught the last rays of the sunset, a tribute to the good old days of the missile base.

It was time for Green River's Rockabilly Night, a weekly event hosted by Howie and the Ramblin' Road Rangers, part of Howie's winning platform as mayor.

Rockabilly Night usually consisted of the band playing tunes requested by the crowd, as well as some of the band's own original ones, with Timmy's Little Popcorn Wagon nearby, a small trailer that served popcorn and slushies.

A long line of kids had formed at the stand, and the park was slowly filling with townspeople carrying their camp chairs, some with picnics. Bud noted the same pair he'd met at the cafe were filming Howie and the band setting up on the flagstone stage, Howie seemingly oblivious.

Bud wondered what Frosty and Eileen were doing—he figured they should be married by now and were probably at some show in Vegas like David Copperfield or Cirque du Soleil, but most likely were at an Elvis tribute, which would go with their Elvis wedding.

Now Bud could see that the cameraman was scanning the crowd, pausing for a moment on Wilma Jean, then going on to Tad, who was talking to someone Bud figured was probably an artist, since it wasn't anyone he knew.

The camera now stopped on some people under a tree, and Bud recognized Old Man Green and Junkyard Goldie talking to the librarian, then it scanned over near some bushes where two boys were flamboyantly holding sticks as if pretending to be smoking cigars.

Howie was now thumping the microphone, testing the sound equipment, then said, "Let's get started folks."

After waiting for everyone to get settled, he introduced himself and the band, which consisted of Maureen on vocals and keyboard, Barry on stand-up bass, and himself on vocals and guitar. They went into a quick segue of *Orange Blossom Special*, and Howie then took the microphone again.

"Welcome to Green River Rockabilly Night, everyone."

The crowd cheered, and Doc and Millie scooted in next to Bud and Wilma Jean, who had brought camp chairs for them. Eldon, spotting them, set his chair down next to Bud and whispered, "I can't believe they eloped."

Howie continued. "Folks, we all know that Green River, the Biggest Little Town in America, has all kinds of interesting stuff going on, but right now it's even more interesting than usual. I've promised you all a big surprise this evening, but before we get to that, I'd like to welcome the folks of the first annual Plein Desert Air Festival and say that we've really enjoyed having you visit our little town, gracing it with your creativity."

Everyone clapped, and Howie continued.

"Along those lines, I'd like to give the microphone to one of the founders of the festival, an artist many of you will recognize, for he's not only well-known in the art community but has hosted a number of television specials, including the BBC's *Life of Vincent van Gogh*. Folks, welcome Mr. Tad Hall."

After the applause died down, Tad began. "Ladies and Gents, I know you came for the music, so I'll make this quick. As you may know, Green River has seen a number of artists around town this week, and we just had our first annual plein air show out at the River Museum. If you didn't get a chance to see it, get on out there and be sure to schedule for next year, as we'll be back."

Tad now appeared to be looking for someone, then, his eyes stopping on Bud, continued. Bud wondered if he weren't looking for Kate and Charles, who he knew had left town. He noted that Will the cameraman was still filming everything.

Tad continued. "We've decided that each year we're going to honor someone in the community by donating the Best of Show painting to them, someone who's played an important role in the lives of the people of Green River. This year's recipient is no longer a Green River resident, but for many years came here and gave his services freely to those who couldn't afford to pay for them by donating his time to the medical clinic."

As he spoke, a man and woman carried a large painting onto the stage, one that Bud recognized as Tad's *Paradise Found*.

"Tonight, I'm honored to recognize Doc Richardson with the gift of this painting. Come on up, Doc, and say a few words."

Bud grinned—it was the first time he'd ever seen Doc flustered. Millie was laughing, pushing Doc up from his chair, and he was soon on the stage, profusely thanking everyone and talking about how he and Millie had wanted to buy that very same painting but it hadn't been for sale and how much he missed Green River, even though when he'd had his practice he'd lived in Price, and how he was even thinking of moving back to be around such generous people. By the time he came back and sat down, carrying the painting, he seemed fit to be tied and thoroughly embarrassed. Millie laughed, taking his hand and holding it tight.

The crowd clapped and cheered, many of them having once been Doc's patients.

Howie, now back on the microphone, said, "And now, folks, it's time for our joke of the week. OK, listen up, because after this, I'm going to make my big announcement, but I have to torture you a bit first as part of my job as a good mayor. OK, two hydrogen atoms meet.

One says, *I've lost my electron.* The other says, *Are you sure?* The first replies, *Yes, I'm positive.*"

The audience groaned as Howie played a little lick on his guitar, then said, "OK, time for the big announcement. Word's gotten back to me that a few of you weren't too happy with my plans to bring in a Cracker Barrel to make sure my wife had a place to shop when the mood hit her without having to go to Junction or Price."

The crowd booed, and Howie patiently waited, then said, "I listened to you and canned that one, but I would certainly back anyone with an idea for a nice little shop like that, maybe without the restaurant attached, because we should shop local. You all know we need something to help our little town survive lean times. So, I'm thinking about maybe bringing in a dairy or a chicken farm."

Howie cupped his hand over his ear as the crowd booed even more, then continued. "OK, OK, I have an even better idea. I hope you've been able to attend the show out at the airport put on by the Desert Wings RC Club, because it was a lot of fun."

The crowd clapped.

"After consulting with the powers that be, whoever they are, mostly me and myself and the city council, I've extended an offer to the club saying Green River City will build an RC airstrip and even pave it, if they'll consent to host their event here every year. Folks, they've agreed to do this, and not to worry, as we have the money in the budget, and these RC shows are great because people have fun and no one gets hurt, and this will help the economy because these people spend money not only here when they visit, but nationally by creating jobs because companies have to keep making all the parts to fix their planes when they crash and blow to pieces."

Bud grinned as the audience clapped and cheered.

"Now, on to the *really* big news," Howie said, beaming in his newfound popularity. "Some of you may have noticed a fellow with a camera filming all over town this past week—in fact, he's over there filming as I speak."

He pointed to Will the cameraman, who nodded his head in acknowledgement as a few people clapped.

Howie said, "I would like to introduce the mastermind behind that camera, or whatever one would call him. Folks, here's Mike Kishimoto, who's a big producer with a certain television show, and he's going to tell you all about it."

Now the fellow that Bud recognized as being the one carrying the notebook around while following Will the cameraman came onstage as everyone clapped. Taking the microphone, he said, "Friends, a few months ago, my secretary brought me a letter from your mayor, inviting me and my crew to come visit your wonderful town. I at first had no idea where Green River even was, but with Google Earth, I was able to figure it out."

The crowd clapped, though only half-heartedly.

Mike continued. "After some research, I found out about your rockabilly mayor and that you have a rockabilly concert every Saturday night, and I thought this would be kind of fun, so I booked rooms for my cameraman Will and myself, and we came on out. Your mayor has been extremely helpful, and I must admit I was somewhat surprised to see how much fun you all have out here in the middle of nowhere—art festivals with famous artists, radio-controlled aircraft shows, concerts in the park, river rafting, amazing canyons, cafes that one visits only by invitation—and I love that idea because it keeps it from getting too crowded—and you even have your own Green River Watermelon Spritzer!"

The crowd cheered, chanting "Old Man Green, Old Man Green," over and over. Bud could see him standing at the edge of the crowd, looking almost as embarrassed as Doc had been, the camera now focused on him.

"So," Mike continued. "After spending a good amount of time here, I've made the executive decision that we'll be coming back with a full crew and doing a number of episodes on Green River, because this is a happening place!"

With that, the crowd cheered as Howie took back the microphone.

"One small thing Mike forgot to tell you, folks, is that his TV show is called *G'Day America*—yes, the very same show you watch every morning over your coffee."

The crowd cheered, then Howie and the Ramblin' Road Rangers started playing a tune that sounded to Bud like the theme song from that old TV show *Bonanza*.

Just then, Eldon stood and folded up his chair, saying, "Well, that takes the cake. Say goodbye to our quiet little town."

Bud replied, "Firmum in vita nihil."

"What the heck does that mean?"

"Nothing in life is permanent," Bud answered. "We'll survive, and we still have all that country out in the Big Empty waiting for us, Eldon, and for Frosty, too, when he gets back. I seriously doubt if Green River's going to change much."

"I hope you're right," Eldon replied, setting his chair back down.

Bud waited for the break, then told everyone he was tired and was going home to check on the dogs. As he walked across the park, he saw Howie.

"You leaving already, Sheriff?"

"That was great, Howie. Congratulations and well done. But these last few days have really worn me out. I'm going to go sit on the back porch with the dogs and play my harmonica."

"Do you feel comfortable with the way everything turned out?" Howie asked.

Bud wasn't sure what he was asking, but replied, "I guess, since no crime was committed in the making of the story, and no harm was done, at least not intentionally. The letter did say no sleuthing permitted, and I guess I really didn't do all that much of it."

"Maybe there really was a perfect crime committed, Bud," Howie said thoughtfully.

"If so, we wouldn't know anything about it, Howie," Bud replied.

They both walked across the grass and on to better things.

∽

ABOUT THE AUTHOR

Chinle Miller writes from southeastern Utah and western Colorado, where she spends most of her time wandering with her dogs. She has an A.S. in Geology, a B.A. in Anthropology, and an M.A. in Linguistics.

If you enjoyed this book, you'll also enjoy Bud's look at his little town of Green River, Utah in *A Slice of Life in Watermelon Town,* as well as the other books in the Bud Shumway mystery series:

The Ghost Rock Cafe
The Slickrock Cafe
The Paradox Cafe
The No Delay Cafe
The Silver Spur Cafe
The Ice House Cafe
The Rattlesnake Cafe
The Beartooth Cafe
The Melon Rind Cafe
The Cessna Cafe
The Klondike Cafe
The Yellow Cat Cafe
The Swiftcurrent Cafe
The Sunnyside Cafe
The Temple Mountain Cafe
The Black Dragon Cafe is the sixteenth book in this series.

And don't miss *Desert Rats: Adventures in the American Outback, Uranium Daughter, Wandering off the Map,* and *The Impossibility of Loneliness,* also by Chinle Miller.

And if you enjoy Bigfoot stories, you'll love *Rusty Wilson's Bigfoot Campfire Stories* and his many other Bigfoot books, as well as his popular *Chasing After Bigfoot: My Search for North America's Most Elusive Creature.*

Other offerings from Yellow Cat Publishing include an RV series by RV expert Sunny Skye, which includes *Living the Simple RV Life, The Truth about the RV Life,* and *RVing with Pets,* as well as *Tales of a Campground Host.* And don't forget to check out the books by Sunny's friend, Bob Davidson: *On the Road with Joe* and *Any Road, USA.* And finally, you'll love Roger Dean Miller's comedy thriller, *Bombing Hoffman.*

www.ingramcontent.com/pod-product-compliance
Lightning Source LLC
Chambersburg PA
CBHW031109260626
47172CB00001B/282